WHERE SHADOWS SLEEP

WHERE SHADOWS SLEEP

Lawrence Weill

Seventh Star
Press

Cover design: Olivia Pro Design

Cover art in this book copyright © 2025 Olivia Pro Design and Seventh Star Press, LLC.

Editor: Stephen Zimmer

Published by Seventh Star Press, LLC.

ISBN Number: 979-8-9861185-7-4

Seventh Star Press

www.seventhstarpress.com

info@seventhstarpress.com

Publisher's Note:

Where Shadows Sleep is a work of fiction. All names, characters, and places are the product of the author's imagination, used in fictitious manner. Any resemblances to actual persons, places, locales, events, etc. are purely coincidental.

Printed in the United States of America

First Edition

To the Amazing Ms. Gish

CHAPTER 1

They were family friends, relatives in some distant way I never completely followed. I would hear my father and grandmother talking about who had married whom, and how that meant we were kin, but my mind quickly lost track of the chain. Whatever the relationship was, it was distant. But they were good friends of my father's.

We went out to visit them one Sunday, far out in the country. I liked them. They were always pleasant, if somewhat dismissive of the children. But they had a son about my age (I was eight) and a daughter just a little older, and together with my siblings, we all were sent out of the house to play and run around the farm and stay out of the way.

The house was modest, but the acreage was impressive. A huge vegetable garden. Pastures next door, where cows moseyed past, their glassy, sleepy eyes keeping watch on us from behind the barbed wire, but not perturbed. A cornfield that stretched as far as I could see, even when I stood on the small porch, taking my turn at the ice cream churn. When we weren't put to work cranking the ice bucket, we played hide-and-seek. So many places to hide: the barn, sheds everywhere full of tractors and barrels to slip behind, gnarled maple trees that dropped helicopter seed pods on us while we crouched behind them.

I loved hiding. It gave me practice in being invisible, and I enjoyed the concept of invisibility, a notion I learned early on. If I were invisible, ostensibly I could do no wrong, or at least, no wrong I could be held accountable for. And I had a history of being invisible. There were five kids in our family, and I was one of the middle ones, invisible. We were not quite middle class, although not really poor, but still, that made me invisible.

I always chose the cornfield to hide in, and they never found me. If I saw the corn tousled from someone entering, I moved deeper into the rows and rows of green and yellow stalks. There were bulging ears on the corn, nearly ready for harvest, no doubt. Rusty yellow and brown silks puffed from the tops of the ears that were above my head. The air was full of the smell of green, bursting with life, sweet, milky. The field was a treasure for my senses.

Then they called allie-outs-in-free because dinner was ready, but I was trapped. I heard them, but I could not tell what direction the tinny, distant voice called from. I was entirely unable to disentangle myself from the cornfield. I swung around, waiting for a second call so I could get a better idea of which way to go, but they didn't call.

I had not been missed. Invisible boys are not missed. I walked towards where I thought the house was, but actually moved deeper into the rows, evidently, letting the long scratchy leaves caress my arm. Then, I knew I didn't know the way, and still no one was calling. I realized, I didn't care. No, it was more than I didn't care: I loved it. I was lost in the cornfield, and, being lost and trying to determine my whereabouts, my senses were opened.

At first, I looked for a path out, but I had found so

much more than that. When I looked up, past the giant stalks with gently swaying fronds, the sky above was mid-summer blue, cloudless. So blue it almost hurt my eyes. Was the sky ever this clear and perfect before? Somewhere beneath the intoxicating scent of the corn was the coppery odor of the earth below it. Could I smell the earthworms within it? The soil was deep brown and clotted with yesterday's rain.

I kept walking, my arms outstretched, slowly passing the gauntlet of coarse leaves. I wanted to hug the corn stalks, catch and hold and talk with the grasshoppers that whirred past my head. If my siblings had been still calling, I wouldn't have heard them over the gentle shushing of the corn in the slight breeze. It was a green noise.

I kept my path into the maize. How far did this field go? I didn't know. I hoped forever. It seemed so. That was what I thought would be perfection, a field of beautifully ripe corn that stretched out for eternity and me invisible within. No one around to tell me otherwise. Just me and my immediate surroundings, made brighter, louder, more pungent by the fact that I was the lone intruder here. I was the one lost in the field of corn. I knew then that it was the fact that I was lost that made it even more intense, heightening my senses to everything going on in the field. It was as if I was let go, released like a too-small bluegill returned to the pond. I swam on through the green field, free, open. The intoxicating feeling of opening up to the world grew stronger.

And then I knew I would never be found.

This was the end. Or the beginning. This was how it happens; a little unseeable boy wanders off and is never heard from again. Eventually, he is missed. Searches yield nothing, but how do you find what you cannot see? Family and friends grieve, briefly, but move on, and then not only is the little boy lost, but so is his memory. Even my memory is imperceptible. That is what passed through my thoughts. This was how I would meet my own doom. But in whatever fear I had was also elation, for now I was free. And then the fear was gone. My spirit flew above me. Dark. Floating. Was that a crow or my own soul?

I stood, almost catatonic, and whiled away the minutes. When I moved, I wandered, moseyed, no direction in mind now, no path discernable, even if I wanted one. How long can a minute stretch into? Forever, perhaps. Now is eternal. Grasshoppers flew from plants farther away, crossing my near-sighted vision like wispy green sprites. Yellow crowned stalks reached to the heavens, feathery at the top, solid as tree trunks at the bottom. It was magical. I had no idea which way the farmhouse was. I didn't care. Being lost made everything clearer, more immediate. It was as if I could hear the corn growing and it was telling me that everything was okay. I no longer had anything to fear.

Then, I gave myself over utterly to the opening up, to the surrender of myself to the cornfield, to the sky, to the grasshoppers and earthworms and the sky and crows and I found myself lying on the cool, damp earth, staring up, but seeing nothing. Maybe blue and green at the edges. Had I fallen? Was the field swallowing me? I thought maybe so. And I was okay with that. There would be no corpse, no body to bury. I lay on the cool ground, the grassy, sweet scent of the field enveloping me. I was certain I could feel the cool, coppery earth slowly rising along my sides. I did not fight it. It was release. It was the ultimate invisibility.

Finally, I heard my father calling me, far off, advising me dinner was served. I stood. I was not half-buried, although my clothes were damp. Was that leftover dew, or had the field of corn given me a going away present? I

4

shook off the stupor I had allowed myself to enter, stood, and brushed off my jeans and hand-me-down tee. I came back. I didn't want to go, but I knew I had to. I liked being lost, but I didn't want anyone to worry about me. Especially my father. Was it possible to be invisible and no one miss me? I thought this was a good thing to try. I would work harder on becoming unseen, yet unmissed.

He was louder and more insistent than my siblings had been. I followed his voice, but it still took quite a while. When I finally reached the yard, my faded, striped orange and yellow shirt wet from the heat and the hike, my father was leaning on the rail banister and grinning at me from the porch.

"What's the matter?" He patted my head as I climbed the steps up the porch. "You get lost in the cornfield?"

"Yes," I sighed. It had been an utterly exuberant experience. "It was great, Dad."

I wondered if I might try to explain, one day, just what I had felt, but I didn't have the words then. I went into the dining room where everyone else was already filling their plates. I sat next to the boy about my age and took a great spoonful of mashed potatoes and slung it onto my plate. Bowls and platters lined the length of the table, all filled with the bounty of the farm. I eyed the fried corn. Yes, I was going to have some of that. Hadn't the very plants that bore these kernels assured me it would taste wonderful? My father sat farther up the table, the end where the other adults were sitting and generally ignoring the children. He gave me a funny look, blinked a couple of times, then gave a slight wag of his head and picked up a steaming bowl of green beans.

CHAPTER 2

I was lost alright. Finally. I was lost in the moist, warm night in my hometown, or at least, a town that I grew up in. My hometown of the moment. It was not my only hometown. I seemed to have a lot of former addresses. Certainly, it was not the city where I was born. We lived in many places when I was young. I was a child of that peripatetic tribe of people known as postwar GIs. But my siblings and I had learned over the years to move easily from place to place like a frog might leap from lily pad to log to muddy bank, moving for no other reason than it just seemed like the thing to do.

At least that was the way it felt to us. We were in school, playing along the side streets and alleyways of some small, midwestern town, and then we were moving, everything hastily loaded into trucks and carted off down the road. We would arrive, invariably some of our belongings lost enroute, wondering if we would stay and become part of a community. Or perhaps not so much wondering as figuring we would not. If we wondered anything, it was when we would move again.

We learned to make fast friends then, and by fast, I mean quick, not long-lasting. Such is the friendship of children. It is complete and unassuming and shallow, as perhaps it should be. Kids make friends without knowing anything about each other. As adults, we predicate making friends by learning about people. As if people might need to apply to be our friends. We need a common interest. We ask, "What do you do for a living?" "Where are you from?" "Where did you go to school?" With children, it can be as simple as there is someone else here now to hold the bat. There's someone to hide from us while we seek them. And then they are friends.

But there was no one around to seek me in the darkness, in this western Kentucky town. It shouldn't be surprising I was lost. I was thirteen. My extent of knowing the back streets should have only been sitting in the rear seat with my brother in my father's long sedan, unable to see out, and not trying to, since we had arrived without fanfare one autumn day and had settled in as we usually did. In fact, this boy who was wandering about aimlessly in the darkest hours before sunrise was unusual in itself, because I often wandered the streets of the city at night alone.

No, I probably should not have been out. But they were different times, less scary times. A time when a child could walk down the street and hide from the occasional traffic and still manage to make it home before the parents woke up, if their parents weren't gone most of the time anyway. I had wandered the streets of this particular hometown many, many times. No one knew. My brothers and sisters didn't know. My friends didn't know.

I'm not sure why I roamed the streets alone at night. Maybe I was looking for something, something I had experienced in a cornfield once. Yes, that was definitely a big part of it. I suppose there was a certain solace to be found in it as well. I could be by myself, thinking my own private imperceptible thoughts, and no one questioned it. And with my myopic eyesight, the streetlights gave a fuzzy, warm glow to all of my steps. If I found what I was looking for, what would tell me that I had found it? Mostly, I discovered myself trying to get lost. I wanted to not know the way home. Only then could I have that feeling of opening up, that feeling I had had in the maize. When I was lost, I lived far more intensely than normally. That's what I was looking for: to be utterly lost.

When I was lost, that was when I found something within me that I never allowed to be released, a kind of enveloping oneness with the world around me. Were others allowed to have this feeling, or was it only I who had to go in search of that moment? Oddly, when I felt endangered, however slightly, it was easier to open up. Maybe it was a strange quirk in my "fight-or-flight" instinct. Instead of running, either towards or away from the peril, I simply engulfed it, allowed myself to consume it. Or allowed it to consume me. And when that happened, I was invisible. In the same manner as a fish does not see the water around it, is so surrounded by it, it cannot sense it, that was what happened when I let myself succumb to the darkness, the threat, the night.

Not that I always sought to lose my direction. Sometimes, I just wanted to walk around in the dark: unseen, unmissed, unnoticed, unheard. They were my "un" walks, certifying my one superpower – to be utterly unfathomed. Perhaps there might one day be a use for my superpower other than my own gratification. But it was more. I wasn't wallowing in my power; I was perfecting it still. Until my abilities were strong enough that I might call upon them at will, they were unreliable. Another "un."

I reached a corner. The black and white street signs read McClarty and Conway. No idea. That was fine. Perhaps soon I might have that engulfing feeling, that sense of almost rapture, wherein I was one with whatever was near. Although at some point, I perhaps needed to return to my home before dawn, for now, I embraced not knowing the way. The east-west streets that were familiar to me in town were numbered, but these were not, and I had avoided paying attention, darting across Parrish Avenue after hiding behind a pungent juniper bush to be sure the coast was clear. Parrish would have been an easy place for a policeman, lounging in his cruiser near the school in the quiet of the night, to have seen me and perhaps been shaken from his torpor to investigate. We had a curfew in town for young people, so I hid.

I sprinted across the straight, dark pavement and kept running for a few blocks. Had I run far enough to be close to the section of town where most of the residents were people of color? We had a fairly clear delineation of parts of town where different people lived in those days. Even then, it was arbitrary and absurd to me. The houses here were neat, simple, square houses with narrow porches under shed roofs. Each yard had a chain-link fence. I recalled that section of town where mostly black people lived also had numbered streets. No, I didn't think I had run that far. At least yet. But when everyone was inside, asleep, how would anyone know? Where was I? I felt my senses opening up. It was coming. Finally. Moths swarmed around the sodium streetlight above me. The light itself buzzed, as if singing to the tiny beasts.

Fenced yards were something I didn't like to see. It meant no running between houses to escape after seeing the wayward flash of headlights from a car turning the corner. Part of the journey was not getting caught breaking curfew. Part of it was that game. To not be seen by anyone. Maintain my invisibility, my superpower. And fences might also mean dogs. Dogs always saw me. Or perhaps smelled me. I tried to avoid dogs because they liked to watch me from under a ramp or behind the edge of the house as I was passing and then skulk up behind me and start barking suddenly and loudly, which both startled the wits out of me and possibly alerted a homeowner someone was lurking in the darkness outside their homes. Which was true.

And I did walk through many quiet neighborhoods. Residential streets, staying away from the few thoroughfares in town on my sojourns. Those were wide, brightly lit, and deserted at night, which meant it would be easy to see someone scampering across the road, even several blocks away. A grown man would have been suspect. I would have been far more than that. I also stayed away from the business areas. There was so little of interest there for me, and there was no way for me to become lost in a shopping center or downtown. I knew those areas too well. I walked on.

Railroad tracks crossed the street a half block up. I could smell the tarred ties from where I was. A slight breeze made dappled shadows along the curb from the yellow lamp above. A dog barked far away on some other street, perhaps at some other phantom walker, perhaps at a cat, or maybe its own moonlit shadow. I had learned that dogs are like people in that way: they distrust their first impressions. Are afraid of what they fear they don't know. Then angry at getting caught being afraid. The dog gave a grunting, cough-like ending to his barking fit, as if adding punctuation to whatever canine sentence had been thrown into the cool night.

Beyond the tracks, something loomed in the darkness, a larger building, maybe. I couldn't tell. My vision was too poor, and it was too dark. I didn't trust the sheer size of it. Too many times, the night played tricks on me, like an impish playmate, setting out traps for me that I was supposed to discover and untangle, but they often deceived me. Sometimes, it fooled my hearing into believing traffic was just beyond the next corner, like a river that cannot be crossed but still points to the way back from where I started. Moonlight made my eyes see colors all wrong. The moon turns dark puddles into shimmering streams of light. Toys strewn across the various yards are grey and black. Yet, I felt a calm, even when lost. It had been at least part of what I had sought.

To have been such a roaming child, a sense of direction might be expected, but in fact I had almost no idea where I was normally. I worked at being lost, so it came as second nature to me. I once got hopelessly turned around in a house of mirrors at a carnival, a space no larger than a recreational vehicle. That was why I studied maps in places I could not afford to get lost, spending hours and hours poring over them until I knew enough landmarks, a few street names that would eventually lead me to where I was supposed to be. It usually worked. I got into unfamiliar ground, strolled around in it happily, then found my way home. But tonight, I saw nothing familiar, and I had walked a long way.

Was I walking towards the Ohio River? If so, I would know when I reached it, but it meant being on the opposite side of town from where we lived. Or maybe moving out towards the farmlands that abutted the city, low flat fields where soybeans and untended corn straggled up behind barbed wire fences. I decided to follow the tracks, figuring they maybe led to the crossing at Ninth and Frederica Streets, the one and only four lane road in town, at that time. If I was right, familiar territory would present itself before reaching the boulevard and I could cut up Locust

Street and head home via the back streets.

But the truth was, I had no idea if I was walking towards that crossing or heading out of town. The night smelled of moisture and a vague tobacco odor that wafted from the warehouses downtown that we could always smell throughout the town at night in late summer. I wanted to be lost, but I also liked being able to return home undetected.

I had been roaming the dark streets alone for a long time. It was what I did. Some kids played ball or read books or painted watercolors. I meandered through the town, in the dark, unseen. I liked being intentionally unseen. I liked being lost. So much of my life I was already invisible, but not by choice. By floating through the darkness on my own, my invisibility allowed me to see where everyone lived. From around a corner, I sometimes heard tidbits of conversations on porch stoops or through windows, quiet, murmuring discussions, occasionally. And at times sharp words of rebuke and disagreement.

I saw everyone's cars, pulled up in front of their homes. Back then, I could tell the model of a car by the shape in the night. Now, cars all look pretty much the same. But I knew a Buick from a Chrysler. And that told me a tiny morsel about the person who lived there. Anyone could be my neighbor for as long as it took to walk past their house. Kids I had yet to meet. There was a stingray bike. A sandbox. A tree swing. Sporadically, I walked past the homes of girls I wished I had the courage to speak with. I would stand in the shadow of an oak, imagining what I might say if I weren't so tongue-tied around them. Some neighborhoods had larger houses and smaller trees. Professional people in the city: lawyers, doctors, mayors. All of them were mine, my friends, my sweetheart, my mentor, for two minutes on a dark street in the tepid night air. But that was only part of the allure to me. What I sought was that feeling of giving myself over to the darkness, relinquishing my ego, my soul, perhaps.

I wore dark clothes on my treks. Dark tennis shoes. I was quick on my feet too. There were a few times policemen would turn a corner and catch a glimpse of something shadowy, disappearing into the foliage. They might stop and shine a spotlight, but I knew how to disappear. They would move on, convinced it had only been a stray cat or a chimera caused by too much coffee and not enough light. I was skinny and elusive.

The first time I wandered out all night, I had slipped out the door of my bedroom, which had a sliding-glass outside door, as did every room in the house. Friends and I had sometimes talked about sneaking out and meeting up and maybe visiting where someone was having a party, or simply going over to other friends' houses and finding a way to rouse them without their parents discovering us and, through such chicanery, growing our numbers. For what, I'm sure we had no clue. Camaraderie, I suppose. But I went out that first night without telling a soul, for just that purpose.

Rick was closest, but he could not be awakened by my tossing pebbles at his window. I went by Sam's, and climbed the trellis up to his room, a means of escape he had used before. He answered my taps on the window with a confused, puffy, asleep face. No, he didn't want to go out. What time was it anyway? I had no idea what the time was. Very late. He went back to bed, and I climbed back down. A couple of miles later, at George's house, I tossed small shards of crushed limestone from his driveway at his window. He looked down at me as if I were insane. He didn't want to go either, but graciously offered that I could sleep in the side yard on a chaise lounge the family had left out, which I did that first time, awakening when the sky was greying, chilled and damp from a heavy dew.

I walked the two miles home, slipped in my bedroom door, and was never missed. I decided after that not to visit anyone, preferring walking alone. I could not be disappointed in their reticence to join me if I expected nothing of anyone. I would walk alone, get myself lost, and let the world open up for me. In fact, if anyone had been with me, by definition I could not be lost, the way I saw it. I was lost when I had no idea where I was and no one else did either. I had not gotten lost that first night, but I discovered how much I enjoyed invisibility. I embraced the quiet, the solitude.

The tracks I had started walking down took a slow turn to my left. I paced along. There were some industrial buildings along the road, which was now more gravel than pavement. Nothing was familiar, but I didn't expect it to be. I was lost and would be until I saw something familiar, which had simply not happened yet. I would, I was certain. It was a matter of time. That was how it worked. Not knowing every business along the tracks was part of it. Perhaps in daylight, I would know these places. I kept walking, listening to my footsteps crunching in the gravel. A street lamp buzzed a block away. The night had turned cooler, and I shivered against the chill. The steel rails gave small glints of reflected light between the rust.

Somewhere in the darkness, a voice yelled out. Was it in anger or farewell? Just a loud, not-too-distant, indiscernible yelling, not completely different from the dog barking earlier, and perhaps it carried no more meaning. Simply a greeting or sounding an alarm or demanding someone or something to leave. There was a sharp pop. A door slamming? More? The sound was to my right, but ahead of me a street or two. I turned and walked back down another street, away from the voice and the popping sound. That felt like danger.

Then I got the feeling I had sought, almost a rapture, the world spun or I did, and then I was lying on the crushed limestone, my eyes open, grinning. Was I crying? No, it was joy. I sat up. I hadn't been down for long, a few seconds maybe, but it was time to go home. I had found what I sought, even if I couldn't share it. It was the purest quale.

I brushed my clothes off and stepped over to read the street sign. This street was wider, and I worried it had more traffic. Crabtree and Ninth. But this Ninth stopped right here. That didn't make sense. Where was I? But Crabtree was a vaguely familiar name. I had the feeling I was a long way from home, and that this was too busy a street to stay on. I needed to find the rest of Ninth Street, where it headed east, then cut over on Independence to Twelfth. That should give me cover. I hadn't exactly become completely familiar with my surroundings, but I at least knew, more or less, how to find a way that was familiar. The exhilaration of being lost started abating. I was figuring out where I was now.

Home was at least an hour away. If I even knew the way. Had I found what I had gone looking for in the dark summer sky? In the empty, abandoned yards? In the windows, dark, save for an occasional nightlight left on in an upstairs hallway? Perhaps. It felt like I had, although I couldn't define it. All of those people asleep. Was that what I wanted to find? People asleep and safe and quiet and invisible? Except for that one voice and the pop that happened afterwards. Now a car turned the corner a block up, its lights sweeping across me. Had they seen me? Was I as capable of disappearing as I hoped?

I ducked behind a battered trash can and watched for a moment. It wasn't a police car, just a faded Belair rumbling along, cigarette smoke and Johnny Cash drifting through the open windows. It was a man. That much was clear. He had a crew cut and a white tee shirt. Everything was easy to see under the streetlights, even with my poor eyesight. But he hadn't seen me, evidently. Was he nearsighted too? Or simply distracted.

At least, he didn't look over in my direction to see what kind of night creature he had caught a glimpse of. He was doing a bobbing of his head, as if he was looking repeatedly in his rearview mirror. Or maybe he was just keeping the beat to "Orange Blossom Special." But I could see him, even if he hadn't seen me. I hoped. The sheen of the streetlights had made him very clear to me.

Ah, the streetlights of my little town. They were everywhere and very bright sodium bulbs. Rumor was, they could be seen from space, although why anyone in space would want to find this particular little city was a mystery to me. To me, the streetlights were both good and bad. I could be discovered more easily in the penetrating glare, but I could also find places to hide better. The brightness of the lights made for very dark shadows, easy places to vanish behind something as small as a redbud tree, especially in my dark clothes.

I took no chances this night. Was the Belair driver the owner of the voice I had heard? How could I know? Darting behind a tired-looking, once-white commercial building, I came out on a side street. The lights were not so bright here because the leaves of trees created soft shadows.

I slinked down the sidewalk, looking back to be sure I had not been spied. At the corner, the sign read, "McClarty." I was walking in circles. Down the street, though, the sky through the leaves was just beginning to lighten a bit. I headed towards where the sky was growing lighter. I found Independence and wended my way over to 12th.

I was pretty sure I knew the way now, and while I was glad to know that, I also felt a letdown. I liked not knowing where I was better than I liked knowing. But it had been a good walk. I had let the darkness overtake me, fill me, treat me to the experiences few others had. I would be glad to get home so my father wasn't concerned, but I would look forward to the next trip out.

CHAPTER 3

I made it up 12th Street to the sports complex in town, where the high schools played basketball and the local college as well. I had been here many times. The city pool was just behind it. I swam there often enough. I knew the way from here, although it was a long walk home. Now I heard sirens. There were several different pitches coming toward me, which made me believe they were different types of emergency vehicles.

I reached the park across the street from the parking lot to the athletic arena and squatted down behind a green, slatted bench as two police cars and, a moment later, an ambulance sped past on Parrish, just a half-block away. The pitches on the sirens grew flatter as they passed. Someone was having a very bad night, I thought. Or morning, now, I guessed, since the sky was definitely turning a pale purple in the direction I was going. I don't think the police would have even noticed me if I had stood and waved, as fast as they were driving. They were definitely in a hurry. I could hear the engines on the police cars pushing. The vehicles sped on, then the engines stopped whining, and I heard the tone of the sirens change again. They had turned a corner somewhere up the street.

I still stayed on a side street, though, once I had cut

through the park, even though the police had gone farther down before turning. Would that have been Crabtree they turned on? It was maybe the right distance. The cops may have had no idea I was there, but I took no chances either. I was walking faster now, trying to get home before I was noticed gone, although that seemed unlikely. My father would get up, drink coffee, get dressed, and go to the office. He would have no idea I was not there. My mother had long since flown the coop. I stepped quickly without running so I wouldn't lose my breath. I remembered seeing the Olympic walkers with their odd hip movements, strutting along. I didn't imitate them. It actually looked awkward and painful to me.

This street I followed now was a little hard to navigate since it would dead end into another street and begin anew half a block up, one way or the other. But I kept moving toward the rapidly brightening sky. When I reached the cleaners, where I had seen my father drop off his shirts, I knew the best way from there. In fact, I wasn't far from one of my friends' houses, but I had no need to stop. I would walk up Walnut, slip over to McCreary, then Locust. I would stay off the main street still, but already, there was an increase in traffic. Folks were out now. No more sleepy houses. Kids would be rolling out into the yards soon. Inside dogs let out to run a few minutes. Before long, I would maybe be taken for being a paper boy. Except I had no newspapers or bicycle.

The sky was almost blue by the time I got to the college, and the yellow light from the rising sun was beginning to glisten off cars in driveways across from the empty dormitories. It was still very early and summertime, so I sneaked across the campus and came out a few blocks from my home. The college was deserted. I was glad to be able to rest soon. It had been a longer walk than I had originally intended. I felt damp from the moisture in the morning dew, the exertion from my rapid pace, and the warmth already starting up. In this part of the world, the heat never quite left the air, even in the dead of night, even when it was chilly. It was as if it held on somehow in the humidity, waiting only for the first few rays of sunlight to begin sweltering again.

I wondered what happened, that all the police and an ambulance had torn down the street to respond to. Maybe someone had fallen. I had heard about older people falling and needing help getting off the floor. They even sold a button people could push to call for help. But would they need police for that? I turned the corner onto Standish Place and saw my classmate Jeff on his Schwinn bicycle, the canvas newspaper bag wrapped across the handlebars that he had adjusted straight up into the air to better hold the bag.

"Hey," he nodded a greeting as he rode past.

"Hi, Jeff."

He had seen me but thought nothing of it. It wasn't out of place now, I guessed, to be walking around. He had seen me, but he didn't know I had been out all night, exploring our little city. He hadn't seen what I was up to. He hadn't heard what I had heard.

What had I seen? What had I heard? I saw dark houses, empty streets, railroad tracks. I saw a man in a creamy tan Chevy, smoking cigarettes and listening to his radio. I had heard the music. I heard a dog. There was a train whistle once from across town, down at the granary maybe, or heading up Lewis Street. And I had heard someone calling. Or yelling. I didn't know which. And I had heard a screen door slam. Or at least that was what I told myself I had heard. It was Johnny Cash I had heard singing on the radio. I had listened to my own footsteps. I had felt my heart pounding when a dog had surprised me over on York Drive. Was that tonight? Yes. It seemed like a long time ago now.

I had started out to walk last night over to Cedar Street, where a girl I had a crush on lived, but I had gotten turned around and lost early on. It was okay. Although I thought she was very pretty, I had only just met her. She hadn't paid me any attention, so I was certain she had not really ever seen me. I was, after all, invisible. She perhaps had no intention of seeing me. I'm not sure what I hoped to achieve by walking down her street in the middle of the night, an invisible boy scurrying around in the dark like a suspicious cat. Or a rat. Perhaps she would have seemed more approachable to me if I saw where she lived. Maybe I only wanted to be on the same block, in her vicinity. Was that enough? If she knew I had sneaked down her street in the middle of the night, just because it was the street where she lived, would she take notice of me then? Maybe, but I was pretty sure not in a good way.

Now I went to the front door of our house and picked up the paper Jeff had already tossed onto the porch, then went around and slipped into my room. But I didn't go to sleep. Not yet. I wanted to read the paper.

I read the paper each day, usually before my father did. Before he even woke up. Was that unusual for a thirteen-year-old? I didn't know. It seemed natural to me. How else could I know whose house I had passed in the dark? I was careful to keep the sections straight, to make sure it looked as fresh as when it was delivered. He didn't care if I had read it first. But he did like to read it front to back. I suppose that was where I got it. I read everything from national news to local news to sports to the comics. Even the classified ads. I wanted every last detail about our little city, and that meant who was hiring, how the local athletic teams were doing, who bought what property. Even who had been arrested and, later, how their cases came out. I loved that every detail of what was taking place was available if only I read the paper.

In my own way, in my nocturnal treks, perhaps I was keeping an eye on what happened afterwards. After people were home and watching *Gunsmoke* and *The Fugitive*. I kept an eye on things, but not really in any protective way. Whatever I saw, I simply saw. I never shared it. And I had only once stepped in to change what was happening, and that was when a kitten was mewing from a branch of a maple, just high enough to have climbed it, but too far to go back down. I knew that feeling. Didn't everyone? I reached up and lifted the little cat, amazed by how little body there was for the amount of fluff, and placed it on the ground. It scampered away without the slightest bit of gratitude.

I had gone back through my bedroom door and even had the presence of mind to unlock the front door, as if I had gone out to retrieve the paper. Then I sat at the kitchen table, reading.

I was just about through the paper when my father came into the room. His wispy hair, uncombed yet, flew in all directions still. Although he looked showered, his face was puffy still from sleep. I watched him out of the corner of my eye, making the coffee in rote moves. Water in the pot. Stem inserted. Basket filled with grounds. Top on. Plug it in. He leaned against the counter and saw me for the first time.

"Morning." He gave me a sleepy smile. "You're up early."

"Yeah." It wasn't a lie. It was early. I was up. I rearranged the papers back into the sections they had come in. I folded it and put it on the placemat at the end of the table, where my father would sit and read, a cigarette in one hand, the heavy glass octagonal ashtray beside his place.

"Sleep well?" He managed another wan, groggy smile.

"Yes sir." Okay, that was a lie.

Today was Friday, a workday. That was why I had been able to sneak out. With a workday today, he would have stayed home last night. Tonight, he would be out until the early morning himself, although not wandering the streets like me. He had his grown-up interests. Women. Drinks. But last night, I had simply waited for him to go to bed before slipping out the door on my own. I didn't go on my nighttime sojourns on the weekend. There were too many people out and I was certain to get caught. Or worse.

He sat now at his usual spot, a mug of coffee and a cigarette in his left hand, gathering up the paper in his right. He set the coffee down, lit the cigarette, and folded open the paper. I watched him. Something about his movements reminded me of the man in the car I saw. That man had a crew cut; my father wore his combed over, when it was combed. But the man was smoking a cigarette, I recalled. I had seen his face when he lit one, although with my poor eyesight, I couldn't really make out the details. As I brought the memory back up, I remembered the man more. I could see him in my mind. I was pretty sure he also wore glasses, similar to my father's. But he had a rawboned look, cheeks red. He kept looking in the mirror. Then I remembered the car had a dent in the fender. I wondered why I noticed that.

I would have liked to have gone to bed, but I wanted to wait until my father got ready for work and left. I thought it would seem odd to go to bed now, since I had told him I slept well. Why would I go back to bed? I sat there in my place at the table, drowsy, just watching my father read, smoke, take long gulps of pitch-black coffee. Finally, he looked up. I guess it could be unnerving to be stared at while reading the newspaper. But he didn't suspect what I had been up to. He only smiled and scrambled a couple of eggs for each of us before getting dressed and leaving. I watched the Buick back down the drive, then went in and lay across my bed and slept.

CHAPTER 4

I didn't go out Friday night on my own. As I mentioned, even our little city enjoyed cutting loose on a Friday night. Or rather, especially my town. There was strikingly little to do in town at that time. Most activities revolved around cars. Drive-in movies and restaurants. Carousing all night from bar to bar in cars. Gas was cheap. The driving while drinking laws were much less stringent and enforcement was lax at best, especially if your family name was recognizable to the officer. There were a couple of clubs in town, the province of the twenty-somethings and thirty-somethings. But for teens who drove, everything was about cars.

In fact, a favorite pastime was driving the length of Frederica Street, from the river to the drive-in restaurant on the south end, a distance of some three miles, turning around and driving back. This went on most of the evening with occasional detours into other drive-in restaurants or to friends' houses to pick them up and return to the route. Cruising. Teens would stop in the street and talk and joke and, all too often, fight. Sometimes they fought because there was nothing to do. There was lots of honking, shouting, squealing of tires. And powerful muscle cars ruled the day.

If the teens were dating, that too was about cars. Couples

27

had favorite spots out in the country, which was never far away, to spend countless hours educating themselves on human anatomy. And many teens drank as much or more than the adults did. There was a liquor store associated with a bar where older teens drove to the window and ordered mixed drinks to go, served in plastic cups to enjoy on the journeys of the night. At another liquor store, one could ride up on a bicycle and order package liquor and be served, no questions asked.

Friday was definitely not conducive to my wanderings. This particular Friday, I was invited to a party and I went, hoping the girl whose house I had hoped to spy the night before was going to be there. No, I would not mention looking for her home, even if I never found it. I wore my white jeans, bleeding madras shirt, and my Bass Weejuns. No socks.

I was early. Another of my weird habits I have until this day. I am almost always the first one there, whether it's a social event or, now, a professional one. But several friends eventually showed up and then she came in. She was definitely as pretty as, or prettier than, I had first thought. She wore a white summer dress with pink ribbon sashes around her trim waist. If anything, she was perhaps dressed a bit fancy, but in this crowd, girls like her made the rules. I was dumbstruck, of course. I wanted to talk with her, but she was immediately surrounded by not only every boy at the party, but the girls as well. Nothing is so popular as beauty. And I was completely unseen. It was my own fault, of course. I stood off to the side, trying to gaze at her without being obvious, although I was. I'm certain I was gawking.

"She's really pretty," my classmate Jane said into the left side of my face, since I had failed to see her, entrapped by the siren as I was.

I twisted my head to see Jane. Truth was, Jane was very cute in her own right. I had known her since grade school. In fact, we were at one time a couple, but only in the manner of grade school romance. Now we had graduated to junior high.

"Yeah," I tried to sound nonchalant, although the ruse was pointless. Jane smiled at me, just to let me know she saw through me and didn't care if I thought the new girl was the prize.

Jane wore a light blue pants and top outfit that accentuated her blonde hair. Music started from a phonograph, turning 45 rpm records that plopped one after another atop each other, playing scratchily the pop songs of the day. I saw my friend Henry ask the new girl to dance. I was filled with jealousy. She smiled at him and the two of them started bouncing to Gary Lewis and the Playboys. She was fluid and graceful.

"She took dance lessons," Jane said. I looked at Jane again. She gave me a smile that said she understood my being gorgonized. "Want to dance?" Now her smile felt more motivated by attention to me, and I liked that.

"Sure." I let her take my hand and we shuffled over to the area of the rec room that had become the dance floor by virtue of having no furniture. I swayed, gyrated inarticulately, while Jane stepped into some of the latest dances: Watusi, pony, and so forth. Jane was lithe and agile, and I felt a little embarrassed at how awkward I must have looked dancing next to her. Even her blonde ponytail swung to the beat of the songs.

Everyone was dancing. The song finished and The Righteous Brothers started playing. It was a slow song, and I didn't know if we should sit down or what. Several couples did move off the dance area, but Jane simply moved closer and put her arms across my shoulders. It was clear we were dancing this one too. I looked down and suddenly saw Jane, as if for the first time. I was doing a weird half-waltz step I had seen on *Where the Action Is* and, again, I did a poor imitation of the dance and was not very graceful, but Jane never lost the beat.

Jane leaned into me, and I finally took some initiative and reached around her, to hold her closer. She let me and we evolved into a swaying two-step that made me very happy. I liked holding Jane close. I liked it a lot. I decided I would venture over to her street Monday night, late. She lived on 17th, near the grade school.

I went home that night in a fog. I had gone to the party looking for an impossible chance at romance with the new girl, but instead had rediscovered Jane, and that felt even better. I walked home, but it wasn't very late, and I stayed on the main streets. I would not be lost tonight. I kept reliving our dance, and the way our conversation changed afterwards. We stopped talking about the new girl and instead talked about school and music and what we thought we might do over the rest of the summer. I was even tempted to tell her about my habit of wandering around the streets at night, sometimes trying to be lost, sometimes just to amble about in the dark, but I decided that might scare her off. I knew it was a different sort of interest to have. Probably more than "different." I might be weird, but I didn't need to advertise it, I figured.

As I walked along the four-lane street, cars whizzing past, I realized developing a crush on Jane was the closest feeling I had discovered to that of being lost. My senses were heightened. I felt a bit dizzy. I liked the feeling, and I liked that there was a new manner for me to obtain that feeling besides getting intentionally discombobulated at night in town. I decided I might dig out my ID bracelet and see if she would accept wearing it. Then, according to the customs of the time, we really would be a young couple.

CHAPTER 5

I was in my room when I heard my father come in very late. He was not ordinarily loud, but he was clumsy after a night out carousing and bumped into doors and the walls of the long hallway as he made his way to the master bedroom. He didn't speak, so I assumed there was no woman with him, although there was no guarantee of that. I turned over and closed my eyes, seeing again the slow dance with Jane.

I awoke early and shuffled to the front door to get the paper. Dad would not be up for some time yet. I thought about getting the coffee ready for him. I had seen him prepare it often enough, but I didn't know the amount of coffee and water, so quickly disposed of that plan. My older brother Leo stumbled into the room. I had not heard him come in, but it was likely as late as or later than my father. He looked like he was feeling the pain of too much partying the night before. I left the folded-up paper at my place at the table and poured glasses of orange juice for me and my brother.

"Thanks." Leo sat at his spot at the table and rested his head heavily on his palms, his elbows propped on the tabletop. He gave out a groan.

"Fun night?" I asked, far too chipper, both because I

was still aglow from teen romance and because nothing is so annoying to someone hung over than bright, cheery people, and what else can a little brother do but annoy?

Leo groaned again in reply. He took a long drink of juice, and just the taste and liquid of it seemed to help some. I was tempted to tell him about Jane, but I knew he would find something about it to tease me about. Or maybe not. I did pour him a glass of juice. He owed me perhaps a tiny bit of a break.

"I have a girlfriend." I said it more quietly than I intended, but there it was.

Leo removed his hands from his face where they had returned after drinking. "Yeah?" He suddenly seemed more awake. "Who's the lucky girl?" His face was deadpan. Did he really want to know? I was terrible at poker.

"Her name's Jane." I said that with a little more confidence. "She's in my English class."

Leo nodded. A small smile crept across his face. "Good for you." I think maybe he was actually glad for me, or too hungover to muster a razzing. Maybe both. It made me smile.

I opened the paper and read the banner headline and my smile disappeared. I caught my breath. My jaw dropped.

"What?" Leo was watching.

"Someone was killed the other night here in town." I kept reading.

"Yeah? What happened? How?"

"Shot." I did not look up.

"Wow. Where?" His interest was perhaps more nonchalant than I might have expected, but then, he wasn't there. Was I? I read on and tried to match what I recalled on my walk and what the story recounted.

"West Sixth Street." I rarely kept my place with my

finger when I read anymore, but I was afraid I would miss a detail. I traced along the newsprint. My finger shook with nervous energy.

"Who was killed?" Leo raised his head as if trying to read the paper upside-down from across the table.

"Says it was a guy named Morris." I heard a small quake in my voice and looked up to see if Leo had noticed. He had not.

"Yeah, that's a really tough neighborhood. I stay away from that part of town." Leo finished his juice, stood, and walked it over to the sink. He was not nearly so affected by this news as I, of course, still I wondered how he could be so cavalier. Someone in our town had been shot dead, right in the street. Right there in a street I was maybe a block and a half from. Of course, Leo didn't know that.

He left the kitchen, and I continued poring over the story. I reread the details. There was a photograph of a house that looked exactly like the houses I was walking past that night. But then, all the houses tend to become the same, after a while. Man was shot by another man after a brief argument. Short hair. They don't know who the killer is. Happened around four-thirty or five, Friday morning. May have been a domestic situation. I looked up at where Leo had left. I tried to blink away my pounding heart.

"I stay away from that neighborhood," Leo had said. Not me. Was that the man in the Belair? I remembered it clearly, although my eyesight was pretty poor. I saw his car, the dent, his horn-rimmed glasses, cigarette smoke, Johnny Cash. Was that the killer? What if he had seen me that night? Would I have been beaten up because I had seen him? Or worse? My spine shivered and the hair on the back of my neck stood. Had I seen a murderer?

I closed the paper and leaned back now in my chair. I

needed to stop reading the account. I looked at a watercolor that hung on the wall. It was one my father had painted of an alleyway in Bermuda when he visited there just after the war. The colors were muted and relaxing, the sky a hint of pale blue. There was a long wall and a gate. That painting was always one of my favorites. I tried to lose myself in the painting for just a moment, imagining myself leaning against the palm tree. I stared at the painting a very long time.

CHAPTER 6

I didn't mention to anyone my fears that I had perhaps seen a killer. I definitely did not go to the cops. I didn't tell my father or my brother nor anyone I ran with. I didn't even tell Jane, although I walked her home every day from school, which added an hour to my walk each day, but I was used to long walks. I thought a lot about whether I should come forward at all. First of all, I really did not know if that man I saw had committed any crime, much less murder. I told myself, if I told the police he had been there that night, I would be subjecting an innocent man, perhaps, to undue scrutiny. And what sort of witness was I to do that anyway? A near-sighted preteen, wandering the streets unsupervised.

That was, of course, a main issue. I did not want to confess my own curfew violations, which were far more than that one night. I had taken dozens of hikes for months all through the city. What would people think of me? And my father? He would be understandably upset to find out what I was up to. Plus, I knew the news would be further devastating in the fact I had essentially run amok and that he had no idea whatsoever I was out. What would people think? What might happen? Would they make me a ward of the state? Send me to military school? I knew a boy who had caused issues for his family who was sent to military school, which sounded too much like reform school for my liking, although I think he rather enjoyed the experience.

And then, what about my father's business? Folks might stop going to him, thinking he was irresponsible, and my entire family could be affected. We could lose our home. And still, it could all happen and the man I saw could not even be the right guy. What if I spoke up, for naught, as it might be, and my family was destroyed? That wasn't what I wanted.

And then, what if he was the guy? What if he was the murderer? What if I spoke up and told them about the car, and what I saw, and he found out and decided he had to stop me from testifying or even making a statement.? He might find me and beat me to pieces. For that matter, he might kill me. If he was already a murderer, would killing a gawky kid seem like a reach to him? Or he could harm my family. I had no way to know this man. If he ran with a bad crowd, some of them might come after my little sister or my brother or my father. Then what?

Was that all rationalizing my own fears and selfish concerns about getting in trouble? Possibly. Probably. I thought about that as well. Was I simply being a coward for not coming forward? I debated that a long time, walking to school each morning and walking from Jane's house in the afternoons, glancing about me suspiciously, although no one knew what I had seen. People in my father's generation were heroes who confronted and defeated evil dictators and self-proclaimed lords. Here, I was too chicken to get grounded for a month.

But then I thought about it and decided, first, my dad wasn't twelve when he went to war, and I maybe should give myself a break on the courage side. And truth be told, he had been drafted. No one was drafting me. It was, I figured, just as courageous not to come forward, to hold within me this perhaps dark secret, in order to protect my family, as well as myself. No, I didn't consider myself any kind of heroic figure, but I did let myself off that hook.

I watched the papers, which was not unusual for me to do, and eventually the story faded from the front page to the second page and on back through the sections until it was no longer news. Then, one day weeks later, I saw on the police reports that a man had been arrested on murder charges. They gave his name, but I had never heard of him, of course. It was so much later in the year, and it was possible I had simply missed the story of the man I suspected I saw, but it was also possible that interest had simply withered on the case. There was no photograph, so I had no idea if it was the man in the Chevy. I was glad there was no picture. And while we had precious few such cases back then, the short blurb in the account didn't say whom had been killed, or when the murder had occurred. Could be a different case. It probably was. For all I knew, there were murders that happened all the time, although they would not have been in the newspaper, since I studied that. Did they report every murder that happened in town?

I decided they had solved the case. I took comfort in coming to that conclusion and, as well, took it as license to return to my favorite pastime, which I had ceased during the months from when I had gotten lost on the west end. Truth was, deep down, I thought I had seen the person responsible. If he was arrested now, my danger was over. But I did avoid that particular section of town. My brother had said it wasn't safe. And I knew he was right. But it haunted me: had I seen a murderer?

CHAPTER 7

It was colder now at night, and darkness fell early. But it was still late when I slipped out the sliding glass window of my bedroom and out into the empty lot next door to renew my nocturnal wanderings. I had to wait until everyone was asleep, of course, and my father often stayed up later these nights, drinking a glass of wine after everyone else was in bed, perhaps savoring a quiet moment alone. Or maybe he was worried about something. He wouldn't have shared his worries with me, of course. I was just a kid. What would I know of the outside world? I knew more than perhaps was surmised, but I kept my imposture of being a "normal" kid.

Outside, my breath made puffs of icy steam. I had put on layers of dark clothes to stay warm, but until I got moving, I was shivering. I was a skinny kid, so I had no natural insulation. The streetlights were brighter, starker in the winter air, and, without leaves on the trees, there were fewer shadows. I kept a keen eye out for traffic. It was too easy to be seen, and the cold made me less nimble, although the cold made wearing a ski mask possible, so I slinked along like an elven ninja. There was less traffic in the winter, however.

I slipped across Frederica and headed through the

subdivision east of the boulevard. These were nice, if modest, homes, brick or stone, primarily, but a few had aluminum siding on them. Some of my classmates lived over here, but I didn't know exactly where. Except I knew where the Phillips twins lived. They were my latest romance, my ID bracelet having been returned by Jane during the fall. I didn't know exactly why she broke up with me, although being young teens, "breaking up" certainly didn't mean what it would later. But that notwithstanding, it still stung. It stung far worse than finding my way when I had been lost brought me out of my delicious reveries. She had her best friend Judy return the bracelet to me before school one day, telling me only that Jane hoped we would be friends. I still wandered down to 17th Street a few times in the wee hours, visiting from a distance where I had once sat with Jane on the porch swing and watching the darkened windows from behind a shrub across Daviess Street, so that I could peer at the porch of my former sweetheart from a safe distance.

The first time I went by after we were no longer a couple, I admit my gut hurt a bit. I missed being with her, sitting on the front steps and sharing our hopes and plans for when we were older. I don't know what I hoped to achieve from this surreptitious spying on her house. The windows were always dark, and if she had looked out and seen me, I would have been mortified. And what would she have done if she had seen a dark figure hiding behind someone's Galaxie 500 and staring at her windows? Scream?

But she wouldn't see me. I was invisible. And even I was surprised how quickly I became totally invisible to Jane after that, despite the expressed hope we would remain friends.

Jan and Fran Phillips lived on Placid Place East, much closer to my own home. It was an easy matter to sneak over across Frederica Street, around the Burger Chef, and up Tamarack to their street, although there was always more traffic on this route. But late at night, dressed in black, I slipped like a shadow along the edges of the yards and found a spot between sedans to squat down and gaze at their darkened home, a stone rambler with their parents' two cars, a Chevy and an Oldsmobile, in the concrete driveway.

I imagined the twins in their separate beds in their shared bedroom, sleeping. I wondered what dreams passed through their blonde heads at night. I was "liked" by first one, then the other, and then back to the first. Yet, I don't think there was the first bit of jealousy on their parts. One day I had walked home from Southern Junior High with Jan's books, and a week later I had carried Fran's, all the time, we walked three abreast. The stars this night that could manage to break through the sodium lamp glare were crisp in the bitter cold. The cars parked on the street reflected the yellow streetlights. A dog barked a block away and I heard it bump against a chain link fence. My nose felt frozen, even under the woolen mask. I needed to move.

Despite the nearness of the Phillips' home, I was not familiar with this part of town, which was an added benefit. Usually, I felt the need to go far from my house to get disoriented, and thus get that feeling of openness, that sense of heightened awareness, that I sought. But all of this area was new to me, so within a few blocks, turning corners in random patterns, I had no idea where I was. I liked these houses. I felt safe with the brick and rock-fronted homes. Each house had two maple trees planted in front of them, one on either side of the sidewalk that made a straight path from the street to the small square porches. I turned a corner and saw nothing I recognized. My eyes watered in the cold, so my eyesight was even more impaired. Where was I?

There it was.

There was the feeling. The cold was sharp. Somewhere, a trash can was clanged over by an animal. Or a drunk? No, not in this part of town. The lights above me and on the front porches shimmered fuzzily in my near-sightedness. My thoughts spun, dizzy. I recognized the feeling. I was lost, and thus I was connected.

I knew at that moment, as I knew whenever I found it, that that's what I sought on my lonely, secret nocturnal sojourns – connectedness. I had sensed it before, of course, but that night, the word came to me. When I was completely lost, when I was unfamiliar with my surroundings, I let down my barriers, perhaps better to find my way, a kind of primitive animalistic response to being lost, in harm's way, in the way that a lion cub, separated from its pride, might respond with heightened awareness in order to return to the safety of the group. When I did that, then I felt connected. Oddly, only by losing myself in the dark among strange houses in unfamiliar neighborhoods could I get that feeling of being truly engaged with the world around me. It was important that I had to do it without anyone knowing. That was a big part of it as well. The singularity of it was critical.

Obtaining that euphoric feeling of belonging required independence on my part. It could not be shared. In fact, I was certain the very act of sharing it would have made it cease forever. Alone, lost, I was connected. And when I was attached, I belonged. Invisible, I fit. But there was something more the openness brought me, something I could not name. This was my community, strangers by day, my unnamed compatriots in the darkness. It was their anonymity that made them mine.

Like so many stalks of corn in a vast field, their houses sat in perfect rows. Like cornworms that I never saw, but only witnessed the results of their labors, paths hewn through devastated kernels, my community left the traces of their lives. Their work. Their play. Even their dreams, perhaps long abandoned, informed my immediate world: a tricycle overturned beside a sidewalk, a playhouse crudely constructed under the bare, curving limbs of a forsythia, cars left on driveways, shrubs, now barren in winter, lining up against a foundation.

These people in these houses belonged to me and no one else precisely because they had no faces, or every face. Because I controlled the narrative, indeed, wrote and forgot the narrative each time I went out. I was free. The immediacy of my experience each time I found myself lost was that feeling of having only that particular moment to live in. There was no moment before. No cause to have an effect. And no moment was pending from this one. Nothing resulted. It was an eternity of time held in that instant of experiencing the now of it. And the space I was in, untethered, unfamiliar, was only the compression of that time. That was the immediacy of it. It was ineffable and private. Like seeing a color I had never seen before. And I could not manufacture it. I could not force it. I could only put myself into the circumstances that might allow the feeling to return on its own, then let myself fall into it, like a reverie, like trying to see magenta. I could not see magenta unless I put myself into the presence of something that was magenta. I could pull out the crayon and see it, but otherwise I was only remembering it, or imagining it. It was the same with my trances of the night. It occurred to me that I would have liked to have had that connectedness during daylight hours, in my everyday world, but that did not seem possible. In fact, it has rarely been possible. In an impossibly large corn patch, yes. Maybe in another world where I was the lone person, letting down my guard.

I had similar feelings when I let my guard down to girls, when I allowed myself to be open, to have that adolescent crush on a pretty young lady, open, malleable, unguarded. I felt connected to the world around me precisely because an attractive schoolgirl glanced my way, smiled, spoke, allowed me to call. But the night was kinder, more forgiving. The night gave me back, with a promise of safety somewhere.

Teenage girls did not. They meant me no harm, I understood, or thought I did. They simply were navigating the same awkwardness and self-doubt I did, although some must surely have had considerably less self-doubt than I, being the very definition of pretty and popular. Or perhaps they also had their trepidations, fears, anxieties. I know now no one is immune to those thoughts, but I did not know that then. I always felt self-doubt, as does everyone, and self-recriminations after they broke up with me. But I went back. I always did. Despite knowing what the results would be. It was like taking the treks in the darkness. I had to go back. Find that feeling again, even if it was fleeting. Perhaps because it was fleeting.

But, the night was safer, with its stray dogs and random drunks and even, probably, a murder. I had my fugue, I gave myself over, and then I came home. None of those experiences made me feel bad about myself. Except the killing I had perhaps been a kind of witness to. Yes, that stayed. But even that, like being rejected by a beautiful girl, faded, and I returned to find my solace.

CHAPTER 8

Idrove along the narrow lane, slowly, the edges of the road being hard for me to make out in the utter darkness, although I did wear glasses finally. Bulky, horned-rimmed ones that perpetually slid down my nose so that I developed an almost nervous tic of pushing them back into place. On larger roads, the edges were painted white. But here, wherever "here" was, there were no lines, either along the edges or in the middle to mark lanes. In fact, the road seemed barely a lane and a half. If I had met traffic, someone would need to pull off to the side, but I met no one. Not even a deer crossed my path. I crept along. Was I lost? It didn't feel like it just yet. I didn't feel myself exposed, open, absorbed. What would it take to become lost in my car? Could I?

It had been a while since my nighttime treks around the town. As I reached my middle teen years, there was somehow less time to do so. And it was very hard for me to get lost any more. I knew my town as well or better than just about anyone could. And unless I got lost, it just wasn't the same, walking around at 3:00 a.m. Was it less odd to wander around not lost than it was lost?

Besides, that was something I did as a kid. I was too old for that now. Except I wasn't. And now, I could drive, and even had a hand-me-down Corvair to drive. Having a car meant perhaps I could expand my lost territory. So here I was, alone in my car, puttering down some rarely used country lane. I might more easily be missed at home, however, the car not being in the driveway. But the truth was, I had no curfew. As long as I didn't get arrested, I was pretty much on my own. But the inside of the car was so familiar; was that feeling even possible inside? Maybe I should stop and walk out into the field. Could I get out and keep walking and traipsing along fencerows until I had no idea where I was? I could, but while I sought the condition of being unable to figure out my bearings, I also did not want to abandon my vehicle along a dark, empty country road. That felt irresponsible, somehow more irresponsible than wandering the streets at night as a child.

I shifted from third to second to keep from lugging along. I had gone out Miller's Mill Road, then crossed over Boston Laffoon Road onto Deserter Creek Rd. I should have been lost. Most people probably would be. But I had been this way before, I recalled. Now I turned left onto a larger road. No, I recognized where I was. I turned right at Oklahoma, but I knew where I was going. Why was it harder to get lost? I would turn right at Ralph and head to Taffy, stop at the general store there and get an RC Cola, then head back to US-231. It was not far. I had tried before to get lost in my car, but the security of the car itself seemed to prevent me from falling into that reverie that I could only achieve, it seemed, when I was lost. Although, as I mentioned, I had discovered falling for a girl was as close as anything I had found.

The result of that discovery of falling for a girl was I allowed myself to fall for a lot of them, and I found that they were often willing to fall for me, if I were attentive and well-mannered. I'll admit, it was hard not to fawn over a girl so that she might like me. So I stayed a bit cool, distant. My girlfriend at that time was a very nice girl named Elizabeth. She did not know about my weird hobby. How could I explain? And, obviously, she could not go with me on my sojourns. Finding that space in my consciousness required solitude, aloneness. I had thought about getting lost together with someone. People get lost driving in unfamiliar cities all the time. But that isolation, that moment when I felt completely vulnerable, that would have been artificial if I had been with Elizabeth or anyone else, for that matter.

But it didn't matter. I couldn't seem to find that feeling again, at least not in a car. Maybe I could go call Elizabeth and we could talk on the phone. It was a school night, so we wouldn't be going out. It was a plan, something to do, but it would not give me that same rush of my senses opening to the world. But I liked talking with Elizabeth. I would do that. But wait: it was too late at night to call her. The ringing phone would awaken everyone in her house. And at this hour, the Taffy General Store was not open.

I chugged along now, resigned to the fact I would not be lost, and I might as well go on home. As I drove, I let my mind wander to all I had experienced in my sojourns into darkness. I had witnessed a few fights in front yards, once a woman slapping a man and screaming while I stepped behind a porch a block away. I had smelled the moist, smoky scent of a burnt-out garage that was now left to fall in on itself, sad, forsaken-looking. I saw lots of swing sets and playhouses that waited for the children to come out. I sat and imagined what classmates were dreaming while I kept watch from down the street, behind some azalea bush or the like. I had heard breaking glass once a half-block away from me while I walked. A burglary in progress? I changed direction to move as far away as I could. And maybe I had seen a man who murdered another. Yes, I had seen a murderer.

I had that image burned into my memory.

I had seen a murderer. And done nothing about it. I still saw his face, albeit fuzzier now even than before, recognized the car, heard the music, and, if I let myself, I heard that pop that I knew must have been a gunshot. I could have identified the car, even if I could not completely see the man. And I had done nothing except cower. I shook the recollection from my head and focused on the dark road.

I had been caught only twice on my treks. Once by an old black man sitting on his porch in the early hours of the morning. I never saw him. He sat in the dark, for what I could not imagine, but who was I to disparage anyone's nocturnal habits? He probably simply could not sleep. I was slipping around on the east side somewhere, blissfully unable to figure out where, exactly, my senses drinking in the surroundings, when he spoke in a low, gravelly voice.

"What you doin' out this time of the night, son?"

I nearly jumped out of my skin. I spun on my heels, considered running away, but that would seem like I was doing something sinister, wouldn't it? And I wasn't, was I? I climbed out from my trance-like state quickly. I still could not see him, maybe a vague silhouette of a smallish man on a chair on a porch of a corner house I was walking by, closer to the house than the sidewalk. I stayed off sidewalks when I could. He sounded old and black, although I couldn't be certain, and nothing of his features was visible. But I was only making an assumption.

"Nothing." I spoke in a whisper in the direction I had heard the voice. Even in my whisper, I heard my voice tremble.

"Nothin'?" He paused, mulling over my reply. "Strange

time o' day to be doin' nothin' out on the street." I heard the chair creak. Was he rising to come grab me? I was prepared to dart back up the street, but the silhouette was still on the chair, simply leaning a different way. Was that a question? I didn't answer. "Your mama know you out at this hour?"

I thought about just where in the universe my mother might actually be, but decided now was not the moment to bring it up. "No, sir." Maybe a little less quake in my voice.

"'No Sir.' You just 'Sir-red' me. How 'bout you?" Had I said something wrong? I wasn't certain. The chair squeaked again. "You live 'round here, boy?"

I didn't want to tell him just how far away I lived, and, for that matter, I could not rightfully say just how far it was, but I knew I was on the other side of town from our house. "No, sir." Uh oh, I said it again. Was I in trouble?

"Where your daddy at?" I was growing increasingly nervous about the whole series of questions. I shrugged, but then realized he couldn't see me in the dark.

"He's at home." That wasn't shaky sounding, but it was apologetic, resigned, timid.

The voice on the porch was quiet for a moment, and I wondered what I should do. Then he said, "You go on home with yourself, boy. Don't be slippin' 'round folks homes middle of the night. Someone be thinkin' you're a rat and throw a shoe at you." He paused, appreciating his own humor perhaps. "Go on, now." The chair groaned slightly as the man sat back. "Go on, get going back the way you come. You come back? Come back in the daylight so's a man can see you."

I turned and walked away. I would have run, but again thought it sent the wrong message. I hadn't really done anything wrong, other than break curfew, but who worried about that except police? And they would not catch me tonight. It took me a while to find my way, but the fact I was still lost did not stir up that feeling. I was trying to find my way now. I wished I could wend my way back to that house in the daytime. I would have liked to have seen this man who surprised me in the night, who spoke gently to me, who sent me on my way without rebuke. I think I would have wanted to meet him.

Then again, perhaps not. I didn't know the man. Maybe he wasn't so nice in the day as he was at night. I wasn't the same at two in the morning as I was in the afternoon. If I could be two different people depending on whether the sun shone or not, couldn't anyone? No, even if I could find my way, I decided it was better not to.

I reached home around three, stripped to my undershorts, and lay across my bed, thinking about the old man I had encountered. I wished I could see his face. I would have liked to have seen him. I finally fell asleep until my father knocked on my door at seven to get ready for school.

The other time I was caught prowling around in the early hours was by a policeman. I had already enjoyed being lost for at least twenty minutes, somewhere off of Foors Lane. The houses in this area were large, new, prestigious. They had wide, manicured, landscaped yards that smelled of recent mowing. The street curved around elegantly. There were cul-de-sacs with yet more remarkable houses. No dogs barked. There were no fences, only the wide, neatly laid out lawns, looking like grey carpet in the moonlight, except where yellow-tinged streetlamps made them greener than green.

The houses nearer to downtown where I usually walked seemed fecund compared to these barren mansions, where no toys, no bicycles, even no cars were left out of the expansive garages. The houses were impressive, but they looked sterile, humorless, unlived in. I had decided to end my walk and go home. It was around two-thirty when I realized where I was and walked across the golf course out on Old Hartford Road. My shoes were wet from the dew. I walked around Johnson's Lake, staying off the greens. Even then, I knew better than to traipse around on the green and leave footprints.

I had just stepped out of the darkness onto Antler Avenue when suddenly bright car lights came on directly behind me and the cop car gave out a singular "woop" on his siren. I leaped in astonishment, my heart pounding. The spotlight was on me as well. I felt as if I were trapped in a cage of light. I spun, blinked, covered my eyes with my elbow against the light, but I stayed where I was, facing the patrol car. I had no interest in trying to run from the police. Maybe I could outrun him. Maybe not. And then what?

The driver's side door opened and a lanky policeman in blue stepped out, flipping on his hat in a practiced move. My stomach had a nervous jitter. "Stay where you are." His voice was matter-of-fact, calm.

"Yes sir." I blinked and tried to get my eyes to adjust to the brightness of the light. He reached over to the spotlight and twisted it to shine on the ground. "Thank you, sir," I murmured.

He walked slowly towards me, his right hand on his hip. Was he going to draw down on me? Now my knees were shaking. Curfew violation was no capital offense, even in this town, was it? "What are you doing out here at this time of the night?" He was only a few steps away from me. He did not have his hand on a gun, only a thumb cocked in his belt. He stood with his legs slightly spread. No, I would not be able to escape him by running.

"I got lost." I shrugged. It was true. I had gotten lost, intentionally.

"Lost."

"Yes sir."

"What's your name?" I told him. "Where do you live?" I answered honestly. "Where are you coming from?"

"I was visiting a friend over on Georgia Lane and was going home but I got turned around." It was true I had gone by to see where this new friend lived that I had met through my best friend. I, of course, had only spied from a safe distance from behind a neighbor's garage, absorbing whatever I could of what his living arrangements might say. Brick, attached garage, Dodge Rambler on the one-car driveway. Shrubs at the corner of the house. Maple trees in the yard. Black decorative shutters.

The officer stood still for a moment. He looked away, at nothing, then back. I heard a faint sigh. "You ever been in a police car?" I felt another quake go through me. Was I about to be actually arrested? Fingerprinted? Mugshot?

"No, sir." I felt my eyes widen.

"Come on." He turned and led the way towards the car. No handcuffs were brought out. I was frozen in place. He stopped, turned, and looked at me. "Come on. I'll give you a ride home, kid." He resumed his walk, an easy, familiar, long stride. I followed him and he put me in the back seat, closed the door, and we went off down the street. He told me his name in a friendly tone, kept looking at me in the mirror, spoke on his radio in a language that was mostly numbers. Nothing was too very far away by car in that town I grew up in, so we arrived in short order. He pulled up in the driveway and I tried to let myself out, but the door would not open. I worried if he would awaken my father. The policeman turned and leaned on the seat, looking at me through the wire cage.

"Listen, son. You can't be wandering around the streets in the middle of the night. You say you got lost. I'll accept that, but in case you're not telling me the whole story, let me clue you in on a secret. You could get hurt. Hell, you could get killed. This town has its share of problems, and the nighttime is when they like to show themselves. Next time, call your parents and get a ride, okay? Don't go wandering around at night."

"Yes sir." He gave me a quick nod, walked around and opened the door for me. I went up to the front door and used my key to go inside. Ordinarily, I would have slinked in through the window in my room, but the policeman was watching me, making sure I got in, I guessed. At least he wasn't coming with me.

After he left, I sneaked into my room. No one was awake, and I had not awakened anyone. I undressed and lay down.

Bad things did happen in the darkness. I had seen it, heard it. He had not exaggerated. That was the second time someone had caught me and let me off the hook. Was it simply too much trouble to write up a curfew violation and taking me home was easier? Maybe. But I appreciated it all the same. That was the last time I had gone out walking in that town in the middle of the night. Two adults had discovered my strange habit in the early, dark hours and done nothing more than give me soft rebuffs. Was it not as odd a hobby as I thought it might be? But I stayed in after that. I did not want to test fate. Besides, I rarely found ways to get lost in town anymore. I was fifteen.

Now I was driving, but not lost, despite my efforts to be so. I turned onto US 231 and headed home.

CHAPTER 9

"**W**here are we?" Debbie looked around her now, as if suddenly we had had a change in our situation. I couldn't see that we had. In fact, we hadn't moved in several minutes. She held her arms open, her hands facing me in the question.

Her curly, long brown hair blew back from her face as she turned to me, more breeze from passing traffic than the weather. We had stopped to read a menu on a placard along the busy boulevard. I was stopping at almost every restaurant to read their menus. Just the sound of the dishes was exotic to me as I articulated them in my mind. It was hot in the sun. The streets held diesel smells and echoes of honking vehicles.

"Rome," I said. I went back to reading. Spaghetti Carbonara. Bucatini all'amatriciana. I couldn't afford them, but they sounded like food I would like. My mouth watered. My stomach grumbled. I straightened and looked inside the place. It was dim, quiet, midafternoon. Guitar music played on a hidden speaker somewhere in the back.

She dropped her arms and gave me a look I could see out of the corner of my eye. "Well, I know that."

"Then you know where we are." I turned and looked at her. I didn't understand her anxiousness. I hadn't told her about my habit of strolling around in strange parts of town when I was younger just to do it. Just to get lost, in fact. True, my town was certainly not Rome. There was a certain safety to that roaming territory. But I didn't feel it was altogether different.

"Okay, wise guy. Where in Rome are we?"

I looked up at the ornately painted sign in red and green. "At Trattoria Romanesco."

"You're not funny, you know," she said. We turned and continued walking along the wide sidewalk. It was true I had no clue how to return to the hostel. But it was also true, I didn't care, although I decided not to say so.

"I wasn't trying to be funny."

"Good. So, admit it. We're lost." She had a bouncy walk that I liked. I had only known her a week, both of us being exchange students from different cities on the same trip, a college-led summer exchange program. We had taken up together almost immediately.

Now, we were inseparable. She was pretty and witty and had a quick laugh. She said she liked that I seemed quiet, but not especially shy, like I was always keeping a secret. I told her I was. She had asked me to share it with her, but I told her it was a secret. I couldn't tell. At least not yet. The secret I could not tell her was, in my own way, I was a perpetual witness. I had, in fact, witnessed many crimes through the years on my nighttime roving about walks and drives, but I never told anyone.

Darkness was the home of violence, I had found. Violence and anger and fear. It might be the best time for me to lose my bearings, but I also knew it was the best time for me to lose much more. I didn't report the crimes I witnessed, although some of them were maybe pretty big crimes, and I never testified. It wasn't a secret I cared to share. For one thing, it would mean explaining my nocturnal meanderings. Who does that? Who walks around alone all night for no reason? How reliable a witness would such a person be? Plus, I was afraid I myself would be suspect if I came forward. Maybe I was. If I saw the crime and did nothing, was I guilty too?

But it wasn't only crimes I saw. I saw homes filled with families. Love and comfort. Was that part of what I was looking for?

I stopped and turned to face her. "I'm not lost. I'm with you." It came out glib, but that wasn't how I meant it. "You're not lost. You're with me. And we're in Rome. What more do we need to know?"

"Well, I don't know, maybe how to get back to the hostel? Where to find the others?" She shook her head and her hair tousled. Her sarcastic tone oozed at me. I liked her sarcasm.

"Well, it's near the train station, right? So, all we have to do is find the train station and then we'll be back in the area of the hostel." I shrugged. It seemed perfectly reasonable to me. It was true I had no idea which direction the station might be, but it was still early. I had wandered around in the dark before, completely turned around.

And here in Rome, it was broad daylight. Cars whizzed past on the street, narrowly dodging tourists who seemed oblivious to the danger they were in. The sun was screaming hot, but that did nothing to slow down Rome. We could hear conversations in Italian going on in store fronts. Couples argued along street corners, or embraced in passionate kisses. People ogling fountains and fallen remnants of an empire. Isn't this what it meant to visit Rome? Wander the streets. Get lost. See how Italians live.

Rather than being a cause for concern, I thought I was doing what we came to do. I would have tried one of those made-for-a-movie kisses we witnessed on the street on Debbie, but I was pretty sure she would not think we should, at least not out here on the street. But then, I might. I mulled it over.

We had ridden the bus to see the Pantheon and Piazza Navona, but then we had wandered around the block, but we had not ended up where we started. I didn't care. I was used to walking around aimlessly. It was exactly what I intended to do. But Debbie was visibly upset.

"So where is the train station from here? Is there only one?" That tone was more exasperated. It is true we had been meandering for a while and we were hot and tired. She had some money and offered to buy me a cola, but I didn't want to spend her money. I had put my last lira in a guitar case of a musician playing next to the grand Fountain of Four Rivers in Piazza Novona.

I needed to cash another traveler's check, but my passport was in my Featherlite bag under my bed at the hostel. As were my travelers' checks. It occurred to me it might not be the safest place to keep them. My father had taken me to Sears to buy the bag especially for this trip. The bag locked, but I doubted how effectively the flimsy lock would keep anyone out. I felt for the skinny key shaped like a feather in my pocket. It was there.

"I don't know. We'll ask someone." I shrugged again. I had studied a map of Rome. I thought I remembered only one main train station, but there was too much to learn, and since all the street names were in Italian, they all sort of sounded the same in my head.

"Do you speak Italian?"

"No. You?"

She threw up her hands. "What are we going to do?"

"I don't know. Continue walking 'til we see something

we recognize, I guess." It was what I had used countless times before, albeit not in Rome.

"And how many landmarks do you know in Rome? We've been here one day. If you saw a familiar statue, would that tell you how to get back?" She had a point. And in fact, the ruins, the squares, the bustling thoroughfares all looked familiar and strange at the same time. I liked that. I liked being anonymous and unseen and caught up in the mass of pedestrians swarming around the city. But it didn't get us back to the room.

I walked up to a woman at a stall that was filled to overflowing with various wicker baskets. She was older than us, old enough to be our grandmother. She looked pleasant. She wore a scarf over her grey hair. She was short and blousy. She was hanging up more baskets amidst the huge rafter of wicker goods.

"Excuse me?" I gave her a smile.

She looked down at me and returned a warm smile. "Si?"

I glanced back at Debbie. I couldn't tell if she was hopeful or doubtful. "Do you speak English?" I smiled again, my best I'm-a-lost-kid smile.

The woman gave a soft frown. "No, non parlo inglese."

I looked at a basket, trying to decide what to do. "Parlez-vous français?" I tried. It was a stretch, I knew, but it was the only language I knew besides English. And even if she did speak French, my command was not so great I would be able to follow detailed directions.

She shook her head sadly. "No, no."

I sighed and looked at Debbie again and said, "You don't happen to know the Italian word for 'station,' do you?"

"Stazione?" I looked back at the old woman, and she was grinning. "Stai cercando la stazione?"

I didn't know what she said beyond a word that sounded

very much like "station." "Yes," I nodded. "I mean, si. Si."

The woman proceeded to describe in what seemed like excruciating detail how to return to the train station. It sounded very far off with a tremendous number of twists and turns. When I managed a peek at Debbie, she was wide-eyed with confusion. Fortunately, the woman spoke with her hands as well as in Italian, and I gathered we started off in the opposite direction we had been walking. "So, this way?" I waved with my hand.

"Si, si, . . ." And then she started back into the details.

"Grazie." We started off. She was still explaining as we started out.

"Did you understand all of that?" Debbie must have thought I was suddenly fluent in Italian. I wasn't certain an Italian could have followed her directions.

"No." I ambled on. I gawked at the sights and walked slowly. I was in no hurry to be found. Debbie fell in alongside me.

"So, if you didn't understand, how do you know where we are going?" She put her arm through the crook of mine, a way to say she didn't doubt me so much as she hoped I knew what I was doing.

"Well, she pointed this way first. I figure we walk this way for a while, then ask someone where the 'stazione' is. We'll get closer and closer that way." I liked the way she felt, leaning into me, walking with her bouncy step. I decided I liked Rome. "We'll get there. I bet it isn't all that far."

Actually, it was pretty far, but we did make it and in time for dinner, but that was partially because Romans eat late. We walked three blocks and asked directions. Walked two more, asked again. And so on.

Finally, we asked a street vendor who smirked, walked us to the corner, and pointed at the station two blocks down.

We ate with the other teens in our group and the teachers who volunteered to chaperone for a free trip to Europe. The teachers already looked exhausted and angry, and we were only a week in. I suspected they already wondered if the deal was worth it. We shared our little adventures around the table, everyone talking about the traffic, the noise, the sites. We told them we had fun getting lost in Rome, then Debbie and I slipped away to an upstairs room where no one was, at least yet, and grappled as passionately as teens can. We had barely finished when one of the other girls on our trip came to the door and looked surprised and not the least bit happy with us for using her bed for our tryst.

"I'll just get on downstairs." I grabbed my clothes and hopped out of the room and tried to dress at the same time. Debbie grabbed her things but stayed behind to dress. The other girl did not look at all impressed with us. She stood there tapping her foot, waiting for Debbie to leave as I made the corner and hopped down the marble stairway, pulling on my pants.

When I got to the floor with the boys' rooms, I went to my little cell (it felt very much like a monk's sleeping quarters) and lay down on the bed, which felt as if it were a large flour sack filled with sand. I pretended to go to bed.

I waited for all the lights to go off and all the chatter to die away. When I heard Big Bobby from Jeffersonville snoring, I sneaked out of my room, down the worn marble staircase, staying close to the faded tapestries along the wall, and through the front doors. I looked up as I stepped out into the street. That same girl whose bed we had commandeered was watching me from the window, scowling. I put my finger to my lips in a shushing sign and headed out into the streets of Rome to get lost.

CHAPTER 10

Rome at night was far more interesting than Rome during the day, especially that summer when it was hot and glaringly white in the Mediterranean sun. At night, it was less frenetic, although by no means deserted. There was no need to disappear, at least in the sense of no one seeing me. There were far too many people out to not be amongst them.

I decided to blend in instead. Become invisible, because I looked like no one in particular. There were groups of people out, but they didn't act the same as daytime crowds acted. For one, they had destinations to reach. I could tell by the way they walked, with intent. They were going somewhere. Or they were already arrived at a bar or a restaurant, where they sat, lounging familiarly in the folding metal seats, smoking, talking, waving their arms as they spoke as Italians do. They leaned back comfortably in the hard chairs. They drank all sorts of brightly colored drinks and, occasionally, beer.

The monuments I passed by on my walk, lit artfully in the night, were gentler, more detailed looking, the shadows bringing out every nuance to the marble and glass and steel. I wandered through the streets, not avoiding people, but falling in alongside them, becoming a kind of *de facto* member of their group, although when they spoke to each other, I didn't know what they said. I could tell from their tones, though, that they kidded each other and laughed at jokes and sometimes whispered romantically to each other. They were just like the crowd I ran with at home. If they seemed to take notice of me, I simply veered off, as if my walking with them was coincidence.

I walked a long way that night. I did take note that the hostel was off Via Torino. But soon, I had wandered several blocks away. I stopped at the Triton Fountain in the Piazza Barberini, watched the water blowing out of the conch, dripping down on the merman and the dolphins, all of it lit from within the water and around it. Daylight did the fountain no favors, in my opinion. I loved it. I kind of wished Debbie was there to share it with, but it didn't diminish my enjoyment at all. And what if she didn't care for the piece. I couldn't imagine such a thing, but not having the opinions of others was one of the great benefits of walking alone, in Rome or anywhere else, to my way of thinking.

As I walked on, blending in, veering off, then blending in again, I fell in with a group of seven or eight Italian kids, mostly boys my age or a bit older, and a couple of girls. At first, they paid no attention to me, as I intended. I was just some person strolling along the wide street. They strode in long, familiar steps up the Via Sistina. They laughed and jostled each other good-naturedly, and when I found their playing to be infectious, I actually chuckled with them, even though I had no clue what they were laughing about.

That was when one of the boys stopped walking and turned to me suddenly and said, "Scusi. Ti conosciamo?" He stood directly in front of me, blocking my path. I had to stop. I leaned backward, away from his face that was a bit too close to mine for my comfort.

I could make out the "excuse me" well enough. I had allowed myself to become seen. I had let down my guard. I couldn't tell if he was upset with me, or simply curious. I was unsure what I should do. This is why I needed to keep my invisibility intact. I had blown my cover, although what that cover was, was mostly undefined.

"Ciao," I offered. Beyond "stazione," it was about all I could come up with. I threw what I hoped was a disarming smile at him, then to the others, who had now also stopped and were watching the two of us with keen interest. I had been seen by all of them. Their dark eyes were focused squarely on me.

"Cosa vuoi?? Perché cammini con noi?" It was the same fellow who first noticed me. Now he sounded angry, and I worried he was going to hit me, or at least give me a shove. He leaned forward towards me. It was a vaguely threatening posture.

I thought about running, but that felt a bit like an over-reaction. Besides, they were as fit or fitter than I was. No, the only thing was to try to communicate as best I could. Try to excuse myself and walk away nonchalantly. I told them my name and tapped at my chest. The first guy looked unimpressed, sneered a little, but a second boy, taller, and maybe older than the others, called him back. One of the girls was nestled under his arm so tightly they looked like a single creature.

"Antonio, lascialo in pace. Sta Bene. Mi piace," he said to the first boy. Then he took the arm that was not draped around the girl and stuck it out towards me. He smiled. I smiled too and shook his hand. "Mi chiamo Giovanni," he said, now tapping his own chest. "Questa è Nicoletta." He waved at the girl within his other arm, whose brilliant white smile beamed out from below her jet black hair and olive skin. She was gorgeous. I wasn't at all sure what the custom might be in meeting a beautiful Italian girl, except what I had seen in black-and-white films with Cary Grant or Audrey Hepburn in them.

She put her hand out and I wasn't sure if I should shake hands or not. What would an Italian do? I decided to rely on what I had learned from Hollywood. I took her hand, leaned forward, and kissed it.

"Ooooh!" the other girl cooed and two of the boys said something hurriedly. The girl whose hand I had just kissed smiled even more broadly now, and although I had let go of her hand she left it there, floating in front of me. Giovanni, thankfully, was giving me a wide grin. He gently lowered Nicoletta's arm, then gave me a look that said, "Once, but only." That was as clear as anything said in English would have been.

"Non abbiamo bisogno di questo straniero che ci gira intorno. Digli di andare via," the first boy said, waving his hand towards me dismissively.

"Americano?" Giovanni asked me, seemingly ignoring the boy named Antonio.

"Si." I nodded. I could certainly understand that much.

Giovanni/Nicoletta turned, and Giovanni waved with his free hand for me to come with them. "Dai," he said. "Cammina con noi. Ti mostreremo le vera Roma." He continued down the street and everyone else did too. He was clearly the one the rest of them looked up to.

I fell in behind them. I realized then my hand-kiss was probably a relic from ancient society and used only in films now, but I did not regret feeling Nicoletta's soft hand on my lips. In fact, since, as it turned out, I was not beaten up by Giovanni, I was all-in-all quite glad I had done so.

I walked along. For a little while, Antonio kept eyeing

me, perhaps wondering what I was up to, but then he too simply took to ignoring me. I walked behind them so as not to intrude again on their friendly talking. I was a guest, I knew, and I should behave accordingly. Every so often, I saw one of the others glance back and check on me. A couple of times I heard them say something very rapidly that included the term "Americano," and they would laugh and throw a glance my way.

Before long, we arrived at the Spanish Steps. The fountain there, The Longboat, was similarly lit as the other fountain. I liked it. The Piazza di Spagna was not nearly as crowded as it had been during the day, but there were people there. I saw a middle-aged couple there who looked very American, the man wearing a too-tight-over-his-belly polo shirt and Bermuda shorts, the woman with a huge purse over her shoulder. They looked as if they could be my aunt and uncle from St. Louis, except they never travelled. I noticed them because the man kept taking photographs with a flash that distracted from the ambiance of the spot, although they seemed perfectly oblivious to that. He snapped all sorts of shots of the water, the cafes, the woman with him in various poses before the fountain and then before the steps and again by the fountain.

The group of us walked over to the steps and I sat on the low banister. The others were standing around, talking. I got the impression they were trying to decide where to go next. A couple of times I heard "Americano" again. Either they were trying to decide what I might want to see or discussing where to dispose of the body of the stupid kid who followed them around like a puppy on a leash. I really wished I spoke Italian.

The camera of the American man flashed again, blinding me slightly. I blinked. Then I saw two Italian men wander towards the couple. The two men seemed to be admiring the fountain nonchalantly, separately, unknown to each other. One of the men dropped something metal on the cobblestone. It rattled for a second.

The American man and woman turned to see what the commotion was, and the second man walked behind the American couple and picked his pocket. I saw him lift the wallet from the man's back pocket and walk casually towards a café. He gave no indication of hurrying away at all. It happened so swiftly and deftly, the man whose pocket had been picked had no idea it had happened. I wondered when he would notice. Probably not until he returned to his room. And even then, I doubted he would remember a fellow dropping a metal clipboard, or whatever it had been. I thought about telling the couple they had been robbed, but I didn't know the culprits. What if I told the man and he chased after the pickpocket and was stabbed? I would have done him no favor. And even if the man was carrying more money than he should, it wasn't worth dying for.

As I sat there, contemplating the moral dilemma, the other girl in the group came over and sat next to me. While she was not nearly so pretty as Nicoletta, she was still quite attractive. Her black hair was cut shoulder length and pulled back in a ponytail. Her eyes were dark, but flashed in the lights of the piazza. She sat next to me and smiled. I twisted away from the piazza and my moral dilemma and faced her more squarely. I returned her smile. If she noticed the petty crime being committed in Piazza di Spagna, she didn't show it. Or didn't care.

"Ciao," she said. "Mi chiamo Violetta." She tapped her chest. "Non parli Italiano?" She shook her head, and her ponytail waggled delicately.

"No." I shook my head. That was easy enough to

follow.

"I speak little English, okay?" She nodded and smiled again, and I thought maybe my heart did a double beat. "Okay?" she said again when I didn't answer.

"Okay," I said, shaking myself out of my daze. I nodded, but I wasn't sure what she needed my okay for.

"I practice English. You tell me when I say thing wrong?" She nodded earnestly now. I could not imagine her doing anything wrong just that moment. Of course, she sought only to practice her English skills, and I was the only Yank around. She certainly did not seem intent on our having a romance. Even then, I knew that. But I decided it was okay if I allowed myself a small daydream of having an international affair with a pretty girl in Rome. Was there anything wrong with a small fantasy? "Okay?" She opened her eyes wider with the question.

"Okay," I realized I kept forgetting to respond. Already, no doubt, she was thinking she should not have picked a boy so dense to try to practice her English with. I nodded. "Yes, 'when I say SOMETHING wrong.'" I used my best teacher's voice.

She looked at me blankly, her face turned into a questioning scowl for just a moment, then she gave me that pretty smile again. "Yes, when I say *something* wrong. Si, Grazie. Grazie. I mean, thank you very much." She said it rotely, as if reciting it from a book.

CHAPTER 11

We ambled through the streets of Rome for a long time. It was easier to enjoy Rome out of the daylight hours. The ruins were lit by streetlights and spotlights that made their subtle features more clearly defined, shadows revealing artfully crafted columns and facades centuries old. Marble squares reflected the lights, giving the darkness a warm, embracing ambiance. Even the homes and businesses along the Via looked more distinguished, somehow. The air was cooler, although the suggestion of diesel fumes still lingered. In open bar fronts, the few still open at this hour, the sounds of glasses pinging off each other, chairs being scooted and stacked as the barkeep closed up.

There were a few other folks out, even late. They strolled around in couples and threes, laughing, speaking so quickly in Italian that it sounded like water running over stones in a stream. I wondered just how late it was, but none of the group seemed concerned about it. Did they sneak out their bedroom windows, or was this normal for Rome, for teens to wander about? I began to wonder if these young people had the same hobby as I did, wandering around to get lost, to have a moment when the world opens up for them because only by being opened can they find their way.

But then I realized, no, they were together and clowning around and not in the least bit unsure of where they were. And I was not lost because I was with them, and, what was far more, Violetta walked along beside me. As we walked, she tested her English quite a lot at first, working, evidently, on vocabulary. She pointed at objects and named them.

"Street."

I nodded.

"Machine."

"Well, car," I corrected, although she was technically correct. She smiled and bounced along beside me. I would have liked to have thought of her as my Italian girlfriend, but she obviously was simply trying out her English. I did wonder if Italian girls French kissed, but decided I was not so brave. Besides, for all I knew Antonio, the boy who had first confronted me, actually was her boyfriend, and I doubted he would take kindly to my making a pass at Violetta. He probably wouldn't like it even if they were only friends.

So I walked along, allowing this pretty girl to test her language skills and happy to be beside her. At one point, Giovanni came back and whispered into Violetta's ear. He watched me as he did so, and she glanced over at me and gave me that pretty smile. Was that to tell her not to kiss me? Or to let me kiss her? I decided not to test my theory. But whatever this informal group was, it was clear to me Giovanni was the acknowledged leader.

We crossed the Tiber on a spectacular bridge with a fortress on the other side. "Thees ees Ponte Sant'Angelo," Violetta said. "Ees very old." I nodded. It looked very old, but still solid. The lights along the riverfront reflected in the black water below. Great statues guarded the bridge, which was lined with cobblestones. A huge round fort rose before us. It was an amazing sight. I wanted to stop and gaze at the view, but the group did not slow down, so I hurried to catch up with them. Violetta waited for me to reach her side, then she leaned closer. "Where ees eet you live in Roma?" My heart did a thump.

"Well, I don't actually live in Rome," I nodded in my best tutor's posture. "I'm staying in Roma." I emphasized the word to let her know the instructional content, but she returned a frown that told me she did not care for the correction of her English in that instance. She had asked a simple question, and I had rudely corrected her. I blinked, gathering myself from this subtle rebuke. "I'm staying in a hostel on Via Torino, over by the train station." I did not emphasize the word, but waved as if I knew the direction to go, which I did not.

Violetta's face grew friendly again. She smiled. "Ees nice?" I felt her hair brushing my shoulder, she was so close.

"Yeah, sure." Had I missed an opportunity to invite her to my place? No, we were only teenagers. This was not a movie. And how would that work anyway? Show up with a pretty Italian girl to sneak into my tiny cell and then sneak her back out to, what, walk her home? Let her find her own way? No, this was not that movie, anyway. In fact, the hostel was neatly kept and very old, by the looks of things. Marble staircases were worn in the middle from foot traffic. How many feet would need to walk on a slab of marble to wear away a fraction of an inch? Huge tapestries hung on the walls. They were mostly faded, and perhaps there to absorb sound and wind, although the rooms, tiny as they were, were cool enough, even in the summer heat. "Yes, it is nice," I offered again.

We walked on. Lost in thought for a moment, I let Violetta step away. She spoke with Giovani, then bounced back to me, smiling. It felt conspiratorial, but I didn't know exactly how. We crossed another bridge, but it was not in any way spectacular. It was just a bridge, although it was lit. There was no traffic. Once across, the streets were dark, empty. We passed the Colosseum off to our left. My legs were tired. Giovani said something low to the others and I saw Antonio turn and give me a look. The streets grew narrower and crooked, jutting away at odd angles. We walked through a park that was dark. If I had not been with these Italian kids, I would have felt frightened. But we walked on, although they did not talk much in the park. The streets here were darker too. The Italian kids grew quieter, perhaps out of respect for the folks sleeping here, or maybe out of fear. I didn't know.

Giovani spoke again to his friends, but none of them answered him. Violetta looked over at me, a rather sad smile on her face. Then, one by one, the group peeled off, heading down narrow alleyways or simply stepping away into the enveloping darkness. Even Nicoletta was gone. Was this their neighborhood? Were they simply going home? But no one spoke, said goodbye. Distracted by the steady disappearance of the others, I turned and saw Violetta was also gone. It was as if they had been abducted by some strange force. Now it was only Giovani and me. He was half a block in front of me. He turned, smiled an impossibly beautiful smile, and vanished through a small gate along the sidewalk.

I was alone. I had no clue where I might be. Somewhere in Rome. My earlier cavalier attitude with Debbie came back to me. We weren't lost. We were in Rome. But here I was, lost in Rome.

The streets here were lit dimly, if at all. I walked on, not knowing where I was except not where I was supposed to be. My heart pounded. There were a few people around still, but they stayed in the shadows and at the end of narrow, crooked alleys. I might see a face lit indirectly from the glow of a cigarette, or hear a coarse cough. Sometimes I heard the sound of footsteps, leather soles slapping the pavement.

I glanced behind me, but saw no one. There were no monuments, no statues. Just dark, sooty fronts with a few steps going up. Cars were parked tightly along both sides of the street, small cars, so close it made no sense how they would exit. Occasionally there was traffic somewhere a few blocks away. Should I turn and go that way? Was there a thoroughfare I should find?

I looked up and saw the concrete street sign embedded in the wall. Via Napoleone III. That told me nothing. I kept moving. What else was there to do? I turned and walked down a block. Another embedded sign: Via Principe Amedeo. There was a park on the corner, so I turned away and went down another block. Via Gioberti. I could see a steeple off to the left, so I walked towards it. This street was wider and had shops along it, although they were all closed, of course. The smell of cigarettes and diesel was stronger here. Crumpled litter lined the gutters and the edge of the sidewalks.

And then, the night opened up for me. I was lost, and maybe in some danger, but I had that feeling of euphoria I found when I was lost, the world revealed in all its intricacies, beautiful and ugly, wild and beaten, loud and muffled. It was a glorious feeling.

Being lost in the cornfield was a revelation. But I never felt unsafe. Being lost in the town where I grew up, I rarely felt threatened, even when I was certain I saw the face of a killer, as blurry as that vision was to my near-sighted eyes. But this was different, or at least a different level. I was in peril here. I imagined the shadowy figures at the edge of my vision planning my danger. I might be robbed, although I had nothing of value on me. Perhaps I would be accosted for no other reason than I didn't belong in this world, and yet here I was, intruding, presuming to walk down their street in their domain. A knife would be easy. I might never know it was coming. But even that did not lessen my sense of opening.

All Romans were now my neighbors. Their homes belonged to my senses. The Roman sky allowed pinpricks of starlight to filter through. I heard traffic, not so far away. I could taste the smokey exhaust fumes from the day, feel the grit of the city in my mouth. The church turned out to be very large and seemed to glow white. It too belonged to me now, belonged to my opened senses. I kept moving forward in my euphoria, turned at the church, and allowed Rome to engulf me. I was exultant.

When I passed through the piazza beyond the church, my rapture evaporated. I saw the sign for the hostel a half block up the street. The Italians teens had taken me back to my room, but they had let me find the real Rome too. I was not sorry to see the hostel, but I allowed myself to grieve the passing of my intoxication.

Through the years, I have often wondered what became of Giovani, Antonio, and Nicolleta, and especially Violetta. I have returned to Rome many times since then, but I have never been able to recreate that sense of belonging, of surrendering myself to the city. And although I glance at the faces, I suppose secretly hoping to see their faces again, there is no way I would recognize them after these years, nor they me. I would very much like to thank them.

CHAPTER 12

The streets I am on tonight are not like the streets of the Midwestern town where I grew up. Nor anything like Rome. This is an eastern city, not far from the Atlantic seaboard, not a lot larger than my hometown, but definitely more of a big city feel. It's not as well lit as the town where I wandered as a child, for one. It has more subtle shadows. As I walk along the dim sidewalks, there are people out. That too is different.

There are lots of sounds, too. Sounds that might have spooked me as a child, but these were normal city sounds. Voices murmuring, sometimes to others. Sometimes to themselves. Trashcans overturning. Squalls of cats fighting in a trash-cluttered alley. Cars revving their motors to make the next light or just up the hill. Or sometimes to gain attention.

The city smells different too. It has an overpowering scent of people who have worked all day. Windows are open, doors too. Sometimes I hear televisions, and I can see their grey-blue reflected light making irregular flashes off dingy walls. I don't know where I am, as usual. Just wandering through the city. I don't know this city, but it doesn't matter. It must be two-thirty or maybe later.

Up ahead, a small group of people sit around a set of

steps that leads up to a fading Greek revival row house door. Another set of stairs next to them leads to a door below street level. A garbage bin sits next to the people, its top partially wedged open with black bags of trash. The people standing there don't seem to notice it. I hear them talking, but they are being muffled, quiet. It's a halting conversation, perhaps more of a smoking break in the early morning dark. It's a sultry night.

The stink of the garbage mixes with a cigarette smell as I approach. I can see the orange glow from two cigarettes, the faces of their smokers brightened by the yellow-red light when they draw the smoke in. The people have deep lines in their dark faces. They look tired, haggard, hot. I keep walking. I don't belong. I don't really look like them. I'm wearing old clothes and a tired black tee shirt, which is not that different than what they are wearing. But still, it is easy to see they belong here. I do not.

They grow quieter as I pass, watching me, and everything gets quieter, as if the entire city has decided just that moment to go silent as I walk past these folks. I have a squeak in my right tennis shoe that I can hear; it's that quiet. I'm several feet beyond them when I hear a man's voice. "Who's that?" "I don't know. Never seen him before." "He lost?" That's a woman's voice. "Nah, he don't look it. He got some place he needs to go, that's for sho!" There's a chuckle, then, "An' it ain't round here." Now there's a louder round of laughter.

I see a bundle of a person wrapped up in what's left of a sleeping bag under the added-on wheelchair ramp at a corner business. As I get to the building, I see the building is a prison ministry outreach. The bundle doesn't stir as I walk past. I turn the corner. Franklin Street. I walk along a side street. There are a few neon signs in the windows, all off, which advertise for Lite Beer and Yuengling. The air has a faint odor of diesel and urine.

A woman comes out of one door and hurriedly pulls it shut behind her. She clatters and fumbles with her keys and glances over in my direction several times as if I might be there to hold her up or something. But I'm no robber. I'm just a person who meanders through the streets all night. She hurries off past me, makes no eye contact. I can hear her steps retreating behind me, rushed, anxious.

I still take my walks at night. It's different here. I don't hide from the traffic. There's too much of it, even late, and besides, there are other people out. Most of the time, no one sees me. Still. Or if they do, they pay no attention to me, which amounts to the same thing. That barkeep saw me, but she didn't at the same time. Surely my resolute gait, my purposeful stride, should tell anyone that I mean no harm. But of course, she didn't see me. She saw her fear. She saw what she worried about seeing.

Is that why I walk? To see if anyone can see me? Is it a test? And what would success or failure look like, if it were a test? Do I want to be seen? Or invisible? Then again, maybe it doesn't matter. But I definitely feel like I am still looking for something in the dark. Or is it someone? What is it I expect to see? Or hope to see? Or who? I always see a lot more than I ever expect to see. Perhaps more than I want. Yet I still am looking for just what it is I might want to find, ambling through dark streets. I am looking for the question first. I know that much, but it doesn't help much, knowing that. How can I answer my question if I have yet to understand what the question is?

I am more wary here in this city. When I was a child, I looked for escape routes from police cars because I was out after the local curfew or, really, just anyone who might find me out. Here, I'm staying alert to who is near, or, should the need arise, where I might escape from a mugger. I could be in danger from someone looking for their own purposes in the night. If I were attacked, what would happen? I carry no wallet, no identification. The way I see it, I have nothing to steal. But it does occur to me that the fact that I am alone, walking down unfamiliar streets in a city I still don't know, could put me in a dangerous situation. If I were injured, no one would know. No one would know where I was, or, for that matter, if I were found, who I was. Still, for the most part, I'm not afraid.

I was held up once in a different city. Even then, I handed over my meager wallet and the knife-wielding young fellow had laughed at my thirty-four dollars I had. Even he, who flipped out a knife towards me, had not seen me. He had only seen who he wanted me to be. A victim. Maybe wealthy. Maybe terrified, although I admit I was not. What was the worst that would happen? Would he stab me? I don't know, but I also didn't know if that would be a bad thing or a good thing.

There's probably a term for me, but I don't know what it is. If there is a definition for someone like me, someone who takes long walks in unknown places for the specific purpose of losing his bearings, of not knowing where home is, of not needing to feel the respite of a haven, I haven't come across it. I'm not homeless. I have an apartment, Spartan though it may be. I certainly have no desire to live on the streets. No, I am a visitor. A tourist, of sorts. But why do I like being lost? And what do I do with all I have seen?

CHAPTER 13

The residences here are not like the row houses I walked in front of a few blocks back where the small band of late-night smokers were gathered, huddled on the steps. Those buildings were inner city tough and hard worn, to be sure, but they at least were brick and stone, substantial. These sagging buildings on Locust, where I am leaning into my steps now, are wood, clapboard, with narrow porches that have multiple splintering doors, each with a beaten-up black mailbox.

If it were possible for buildings to look exhausted, this is what it would look like. The mailboxes are squeezed one after another along skinny porches. Strips of white paper taped to each tell who will not be receiving anything worth receiving in the mail. They aren't getting checks. Not here. And no one writes letters. Everyone has a phone and everyone texts, using abbreviations and emoticons to keep it even shorter, less personal. Less human. This is a poor neighborhood. No one here is likely a homeowner. They are small rental units, crammed together in tiny slips of apartments. "Studios" would be the technical term, probably, but the term, meager as it is, glorifies these hovels.

Even from outside, they look very rough. The few doors with window spots have unpainted greying plywood instead of glass. Most of the doors are plain, unadorned wood. The porches also need paint. Concrete block steps that lead to the decaying wood stoops are half-sunken into what little soil is before the buildings. Stray weeds splay out from beside the cinderblocks. No one is outside at this hour. There is occasionally a chair, usually looking like it has been taken from a dinette set or from some other purpose, sitting at whatever angle the last sitter left it in. The chairs are torn, scratched, also exhausted. Only occasionally will there be a child's toy left out. Are they afraid they might be stolen, or perhaps they have been? Maybe no one here has children.

A car goes by, fast, grumbling loudly, leaving a quick gust of stale air, the scent of gasoline and oil. I can tell it is a car that needs attention, just from the smell of the exhaust. The car slows, one taillight coming on from braking, and they turn down the cross street. Or alleyway. There was no turn signal, but then, there was also no traffic. I scuff onward.

I see two lumbering figures scurrying next to the buildings across the street from me, identical to the buildings on this side: spent, forlorn. The two men, hulking, awkward, are hurrying in a way that says they are unaccustomed to speeding up: limping perhaps, or just so stiff they look like they might trip and fall at any moment. They are stumbling along the wooden porches, perhaps trying to stay away from the street, but the clunking of their shoes on the hollow planks makes them very noticeable.

"God dammit, Jerry, let go." It's a man's voice, hoarse, gruff. I look over and see one of the men trying to remove the other one's hand from his shoulder.

"We gotta git, Carl. C'mon." They both are stumbling, maybe drunk, but maybe a lot more. The one evidently named Jerry looks back up the street they have run down, and in looking back, sees me. "Goddam, lookit over 'ere." He still has the fabric of the coat in his hand and pulls on it. Carl falls backwards but not to the ground, just stumbling.

Jerry stops, and so does Carl. They stand there, swaying under the influence of something, looking at me.

I keep walking. I'm old now, but maybe I can outrun these clumsy louts. Maybe. If it came to it, I suppose I might need to bet my life on that. I'm directly across the street from them. I don't turn my head, as if I never even noticed them, but I can tell they aren't buying it. The smaller one steps off the porch. He still outweighs me by forty pounds and is maybe twenty years younger. If I have to fight, tonight might be the night I find some sort of final rapture. Would I embrace that? I am fearful, I am lost, but I don't feel that sense of euphoria. I think that's a good thing.

I hear a siren in the near distance. Back downtown. I glance backwards. Jerry and Carl are on a flat run at a pace I find surprising. But they are running away from me, away from the sirens. I breathe more easily. I didn't realize how short my breaths had become.

Now I think about the sirens in front of me now that I have turned a corner. I find myself hoping it isn't related to the people I saw earlier, the small band of smokers sitting on the steps of the row house. Now that I'm not fearful of the two oafs, Carl and Jerry, I find myself worrying for those people ever so slightly. They are, or were, after all, my neighbors, at least for the time it took for me to pass. And they certainly did not threaten me, or even harass me. That is how I view them now. Neighbors who are passers-by. They had noticed me. I had seen them. That was as much as I had from my neighbors when I lived in the suburbs in a southern city in my thirties.

My life then was drive home and go inside. Get up the

next day, go get in the car, and drive off. I had at least heard these people's voices. I tried to remember if I had heard the voices of my neighbors back in the suburbs. Maybe. I perhaps overheard them talking to each other, much like I had heard the folks earlier talking about me. But indistinctly. I would never know what subject my suburban neighbors discussed. They were farther away. Their conversation might also have been about me, for all I knew. It was possible they had even noticed me leaving my split-level after midnight to stroll aimlessly toward town. I wonder.

I hear a car horn back downtown. It's from the same direction as the siren, which stopped blaring several blocks from where I walk now. Walking in the suburbs was different. In many ways, it was easier to become lost, since there were fewer landmarks. The houses looked so similar, and the streets were aligned in the same fashion. I recall walking to the top of a small rise in a street and seeing a long expanse of identical roof lines stretching out across the horizon. There was almost never any traffic in the early morning hours in the 'burbs. It was quiet and same and uneventful. In that way, those walks were far less satisfying than these walks today in this city.

The street here is dirty. Clumps of crabgrass grow between the concrete slabs of the pavement. Trash lies scattered in the gutter, red plastic cups, split open, scraps of wadded-up paper. I see a rat scurrying into a street drain. Cars are parked along the street. Beaters, every last one. The air has a gritty texture to it that I can feel between my teeth. I can smell the fetid odor of stagnant water somewhere. I walk past. Steady. Telling the lie that I am walking with purpose, that I have someplace to be.

I am still thin, although I am old now. I am glad I no longer feel the need to hide because I am long past nimble enough to make quick escapes. I lean forward when I walk to relieve the pressure in my back from a lifetime of marching up and down streets, old dusty country roads, cornfields. Always walking. Usually in the dark, but not always.

I reach a stop sign and turn towards where the ambulance had gone, because that is closer to my small apartment, and because I think I want to check on the people I passed earlier. Do I? I think I do.

My apartment is temporary, but isn't everything, when we think about it? I have very little furniture. Just the bare minimum: a table with two chairs, one of which holds my coat for when it grows cooler. A blue, plastic-covered couch. A side table and a lamp I picked up at a thrift shop, so that the fluorescent lights above are not my only light. The kitchen is the same room. Functional, and that's all I want. I do have a separate bedroom with a bed, a tiny side table, a three-drawer chest. Closet, bath, that's it. No television or radio. No wall art. No curtains, but working blinds.

But even as plain as it is, I know I have more than many. Yes, I could buy a poster for the wall, or even an artificial plant to give the illusion of life in my surroundings, but that is only creating an illusion, and for whom would I want to make that image? Images are temporary. Years ago, I forsook the split-level for something smaller, plainer, less trouble. And I moved here, where I know no one, so I can walk.

I hear another siren now, but it isn't moving with the same urgency as the first. I turn onto a cross street. Around a corner, several blocks up, I see flashing lights. Blue and white. Also red and white. The lights break the darkness, blinding me for a moment. I turn and walk towards the lights. It is near where my neighbors were. It is also on my route home, which I only now begin to recognize, and it is getting to the time I need to get back.

I am trudging uphill now, towards the central business district. There are a few cars driving along parallel roads to the one I am on. When I get back, I will sleep for two hours, maybe three. Then I can shower and drink a cup of very strong coffee and go into the office. There I will push a stack of papers from one side of the desk to the other, one sheet at a time. It is its own kind of morass, not the same as wandering dark streets, but just as capable of allowing me to be lost. Most people might call it drudgery, but I don't.

I make sure the department gets credit for the value added by our participation in a variety of projects, and value added means paperwork. And I can do that alone, in my little square office in the interior of the building. No windows. Just blank walls. An old wood chipped-up desk. A vinyl swivel chair. A phone that doesn't ring. I think it functions; it's just that no one calls. That's a good thing. A call means I missed something, or I forgot to stamp something. No calls means all is good. And I am thorough in my work, not that the job is hard. It's absurdly easy, in fact, yet every so often, someone is being let go for incompetence.

Up ahead, I see the emergency vehicles. They are stopped right where the smokers were gathered. The trash dumpsters still reek. I can just make out one of the men I had seen earlier who seems to be talking with a policeman. Behind them, no, this side of them, a gurney is being wheeled towards the EMT van that is also parked there. The bumps under the sheet tell me there's a body, completely covered by the sheet. No one is hurrying. One of the men I walked past earlier is nodding in an exaggerated movement and the policeman is scribbling in a notebook. I'm still a half-block away, but I keep approaching the scene. It is, after all, the way to my apartment.

"Hey!" I hear the man call out. "That man? Over yonder?" I can see he's pointing towards me. The policeman turns his head to face me, but not his body. "He was here before. Ask him." The man's voice has risen in pitch. "Ask him what he seen. I ain't lyin' to you."

The policeman looks back at the man, says, "Stay here," then turns and strides towards me. Even in my youth, I would not have been able to be invisible in this scenario. He's definitely coming towards me. I keep walking. We meet just a few steps away from where the police car still sits at an angle, the radio squawking within, the driver's side door open. The ambulance now pulls away and the lights on the back panel go off. The scene is darker now, but the blue flashing lights are still there. The policeman steps into my path and I stop in my tracks.

"Excuse me, sir," he says, his hand in a stop position. "May I have a word?"

He's so polite, I would have stopped even if he were not an officer. I look at the route the ambulance has driven off. Under the wooden ramp where I had seen the person sleeping earlier there is now only a threadbare sleeping bag. I look back. "Yes sir?" But I think I know.

"May I see your identification?" The policeman is holding a small pad of paper that he is focused on.

"No, I'm sorry. I don't carry a wallet at night."

He looks back at me, as if trying to decipher a riddle. "Oh? What's your name, sir?" I tell him. He writes it down. "What are you doing out here tonight?"

"Just taking a walk, sir."

He looks around at the dilapidated buildings, the trash-cluttered gutters. "Here?" He looks at me again. "At this hour of the night?"

"Yes sir." I shrug. "It's just something I do." If that

sounds like an apology, I suppose it is.

"No wallet," he grunts, scribbling. Then he stops. "Well, maybe not a bad idea." He pauses. Now his face is tilted, curious. "You should still carry identification. You don't look like you live around here."

I wonder what the difference is. What is it about me that doesn't fit? I'm not dressed in any way ornately. My clothes don't have holes in them. Is that the difference? But no, I can't argue his point: I don't fit. In many ways, I never have. But I am also not invisible.

"Well, I'm just staying here for a few months. I'm doing a temporary job at the bank." I point at the building a block up where they have put me up, an older building that they claimed had been reclaimed and gentrified, but in fact has been cheaply plastered over and repainted, with floors that are uneven, cracking wallboards, and unreliable stairs going up to my third-floor walkup. "I'm staying up there." He turns and follows the direction I'm pointing, then looks back at me. He wears a face of apology. "Such as it is."

"You really shouldn't be walking around here at night," he offers. I look over at the first man he had been questioning, who is dutifully waiting as instructed. The officer sees my glance. "He's local. We know him."

"Okay." I'm not sure what I'm supposed to do with that tidbit.

The policeman returns his attention to me. "You walk by here earlier?"

"I did," I nod.

"You see that man?"

"I did," I repeat.

Now the policeman looks intrigued. "And what was he doing?"

"Smoking a cigarette with some other people."

"How many people?" He scribbles.

"Three," I say. He looks up. "Including that fellow." I nod towards the other man. "One was a woman."

"Yeah, what did she look like."

"I don't know. It was dark."

"How do you know it was a woman?"

"I heard her speak."

"About what?"

"Well, me." I throw up my hands a little in a surrender.

"What did she say?"

"Oh, just the same thing you said, really, how I don't look like I am from around here."

The policeman nods, agreeing. "You see anyone else?"

I know what the question is. "I saw someone under the ramp there." I gesture with my chin in the direction of the prison ministry.

"Yeah? And?" It's late. The policeman would love to wrap this up.

"I figured he was asleep." I look over at the drab green sleeping bag, not much more than a child's blanket. "Guessing it was more than sleeping?"

"See anyone interact with him? Talk with him?" The officer suddenly seems tired.

"No. Like I said, I saw some folks sitting there on a stoop, smoking, talking. It didn't seem like they were concerned about whoever was under the ramp." I look back at the other man who stands, fidgety, but waiting. "I figured maybe it was someone who slept there regularly."

"Yeah." The officer glances up. "Asleep with multiple stab wounds." He gives me a momentary baleful glance, then turns towards the other man but says to me, "Stay here a minute." He takes long strides back to the other fellow.

He speaks to the other man, but his back is to me so I

can't make it out, but the other man says loudly, "I didn't do nothing to Daryl. Daryl was my friend. I didn't do nothin'." He looks at me. "He say I stab Daryl? You," he calls out to me. "Hey."

But the policeman speaks, calmly, and the man pipes down.

"Damned straight I ain't done nothin'." He's not looking angrily at me anymore. "I know who did it. Yes sir, I bet I know." The policeman turns his head, as if remembering something and comes back to me.

"You see anyone else out tonight, while you were talking a walk?" He says the last part as if he's quoting me. I would not have been surprised if he had done air quotes.

My first thought is to say I did not, because generally, I never do. And even if I did, I never have told anyone anything about the things I see. But I did see someone. I saw two men who looked drunk or stoned and very suspicious. I was frightened of them, and generally, I am not afraid of whatever might become of me. Why is that?

My mind goes back to a tan Belair with a dent in the fender, a man with horn-rimmed glasses and a crewcut, smoking a cigarette, listening to Johnny Cash. I saw him. He scared me. I had said nothing and justified it to myself, but I never forgot that feeling that I had done nothing in the face of that night. I had made myself invisible to the authorities and, more, to society. I had cowered under the impression what I was doing was a personal adventure. But I had used my invisibility to keep from providing evidence. I had evidence, and I hoarded it as if it belonged to me, but it didn't.

I speak up, perhaps more deliberately than I might have. "Yes, as a matter of fact, I did, officer. On Locust Street." I half-turn my body to motion with my thumb. "I saw two men, running, or more accurately, stumbling around on the porches. They looked drunk or something."

"Yeah, that's the fellas," the other man says. "I'm telling you."

"You see their faces?" The policeman ignores the unsolicited contribution.

"No, not really, but I could hear them. Called each other Jerry and Carl."

"Them Barlow brothers. I tole you." Now the other man is yelling. "Daryl and Carl done got in a fight yest-i-dee. Daryl whupped him."

"Okay, James, hold on." The policeman looks over, then back at me. "You mind stepping over here so I can talk to you both?" He walks away. I'm thinking he already is talking to us both, but I simply follow him over to James. "So Daryl and Carl fought?"

'Ooh, yes sir," James shakes his head. "It was a big ol' fight."

"What were they fighting about?" The officer continues to scribble in his notebook.

"Oh well, I can't rightly say," James is suddenly subdued. The officer looks up at him. "What was it, James?"

"Well," James stalls.

"James?" It's something between a question and a demand.

James's body drops. "Drugs. They was fighting over drugs. Carl wanted some stuff Daryl was sellin', but he didn't want to pay. Tried to grab it from him, but Daryl, he don't get mad much, but he didn't like that. No sir-ee. He whupped him good."

The policeman nods, knowingly. "You said they looked drunk?" Now he's asking me.

"Yeah, but also kind of wild, like they couldn't keep

their balance."

"Well, not too hard to see what's going on here." The policeman flips shut his notebook and looks at me. "Think you can identify the two men you saw?"

"Maybe. I can try."

"James," he turns his body to face James. "Don't leave town."

James gives him a look. "Now just where in the hell you think I'm going?"

The policeman gets a small smile, then returns to his cruiser. I look over at James. He's looking at me. We nod. And I go back to my shabby apartment. Back in my apartment, I feel that familiar fugue state coming over me. In my apartment, sitting on my vinyl couch, I find myself connecting with the world. The blue vinyl looks iridescent. The faux wood flooring shows off its grains. The overhead fluorescent light makes everything glaringly bright. I'm not lost. I have found what I sought.

I know the question.

CHAPTER 14

I know now what it was I was looking for in all these years of wandering around, lost. Or if not lost yet, trying to be. I know what called me to seek out the hidden corners of every place I lived and even visited, almost since I was old enough to walk.

Evidence.

Evidence of me in that moment I was able to take in my surroundings without filter. That was when I knew I existed, when I knew my invisibility was the illusion. I was most visible when I was most open to discovery.

ABOUT THE AUTHOR

Lawrence has seven books in print, five novels, one memoir, and one nonfiction. He has a contract for three more. He writes literary novels, short fiction, non-fiction articles and books, creative non-fiction, and poetry.

His work has appeared in a wide range of local, regional, and national journals. He also is a visual artist working in graphite, oils, metal and wood. Dr. Weill lives in the woods in Kentucky overlooking a beaver pond next to a wildlife preserve. He is also an avid outdoorsman and gardener.